"R.J.'s storytelling feels as natural as James Patterson's, and the short-chapter setup is the literary answer to Lay's potato chips: you just want one more and before you know it, you've gone through the whole thing.

- **David Bashore**
The Times-News, Twin Falls, ID

"R.J. Patterson does a fantastic job at keeping you engaged and interested. I look forward to more from this talented author."

- *Aaron Patterson*
bestselling author of SWEET DREAMS

DEAD SHOT

"Small town life in southern Idaho might seem quaint and idyllic to some. But when local newspaper reporter Cal Murphy begins to un-cover a series of strange deaths that are linked to a sticky spider web of deception, the lid on the peaceful town is blown wide open. Told with all the energy and bravado of an old pro, first-timer R.J. Patterson hits one out of the park his first time at bat with *Dead Shot*. It's that good."

- *Vincent Zandri*
bestselling author of THE REMAINS

"You can tell R.J. knows what it's like to live in the newspaper world, but with *Dead Shot*, he's proven that he also can write one heck of a murder mystery. With a clever plot and characters you badly want to succeed, he is on his way to becoming a new era James Patterson."

- *Josh Katzowitz*
NFL writer for CBSSports.com
& author of Sid Gillman: Father of the Passing Game

"Patterson has a mean streak about a mile wide and puts his two main characters through quite a horrible ride, which makes for good reading."

- *Richard D., reader*

OTHER TITLES BY
R.J. PATTERSON

Cal Murphy Thrillers
Dead Shot
Dead Line
Better off Dead
Dead in the Water
Dead Man's Curve
Dead and Gone
Dead Wrong
Dead Man's Land
Dead Drop
Dead to Rights
Dead End

James Flynn Thrillers
The Warren Omissions
Imminent Threat
The Cooper Affair
Seeds of War

Brady Hawk Thrillers
First Strike
Deep Cover
Point of Impact
Full Blast
Target Zero
Fury
State of Play
Siege
Seek and Destroy
Into the Shadows
Hard Target

SIEGE

A Brady Hawk novel

R.J.
PATTERSON

Siege
© Copyright 2017 R.J. Patterson

First Print Edition 2017

Cover Design by Books Covered

Published in the United States of America
Green E-Books
Boise Idaho 83713

For Dave Mondt, a fiercely
loyal friend and a great American

CHAPTER 1

Istanbul, Turkey

BRADY HAWK TUGGED HIS PANTS LEG down and smoothed it out, better disguising the knife holster strapped around his ankle. With a gun tucked in the belt behind his back, he put on his jacket and grabbed the stack of laundered clothes scheduled for delivery to Ahmet Polat. A well-placed asset within The Chamber, Polat had reported to Blunt for several years before the agency became the target of the U.S. government instead of serving as a more discreet approach to handling terrorists. However, Polat was in danger.

Two weeks prior, Polat went to meet with his handler in a local park when he was gunned down at midday. Women and children scurried away in search of cover as the handler's bullet-riddled body slumped to the ground. Polat had yet to make visual contact and give the signal to initiate the exchange, something he was relieved never happened after observing the carnage. He spun on his heels and hustled in the opposite direction, hoping he never again crossed paths with the people who created chaos in the park, obviously unconcerned with making a scene as long as they hit the target.

There were secondary and tertiary protocols in the event of a breach in the pipeline. Polat still possessed valuable information that needed to be passed on, yet all he could do was wait for the next set of procedures to be activated. According to Blunt, patience wasn't one of Polat's stronger virtues, and the Firestorm chief feared if time dragged on without any contact, Polat might miss the window to pass on what he'd learned and ultimately pay a steep price. Blunt determined not to let either of those hypotheticals become reality and sent Hawk to Istanbul to see if he could salvage the situation.

Hawk stepped out of the back of the truck and went through the motions of locking it up. But it was an act in case he was being watched by either street thugs or one of The Chamber's spies. Giving every indication that he was nothing more than a delivery man dropping off dry cleaned suits, Hawk kept his head down as he marched up the steps to Polat's second-story apartment. But when Hawk knocked on the door, it opened farther with each thump from his fist.

Hawk pushed his glasses up on his nose.

"It appears to be open," Hawk whispered.

Listening in on his channel were his handler, Alex Duncan, and the newest member of the Firestorm team, Shane Samuels.

"Do not go in, Hawk," Samuels said. "I repeat: Do not go in. Protocol dictates we abandon all attempts to make contact."

Forget protocol.

"Hello?" Hawk said as he ventured inside. "Mr. Polat? Are you home?"

"What was it about 'do not go in' that you didn't understand?" Samuels squawked in Hawk's ear over the comlink.

Hawk dropped the bag of clothes on the floor by the door and snatched the gun from the back of his pants. Training his weapon in front of him, Hawk cleared the first three rooms before he heard the faint sound of a board creaking coming from down the hall. Hawk slowed his breathing and crept quietly toward the noise.

Once he reached the next doorway, he eased inside quickly to find a tossed study. Books and file papers strewn across the floor, chairs overturned, windows opened while curtains flapped in the breeze.

Either Ahmet Polat was a messy genius or someone was here looking for something—Hawk couldn't decide which one. The chair was facing the window, and Hawk cautiously reached forward to investigate. Slumped in the chair with two bullets to the chest and one to his forehead was Polat.

"Are you getting this, Alex?" Hawk whispered.

"Unfortunately, I am," she said. "It's all coming through crystal clear from your body cam. I'm running this through facial recognition to confirm, but that looks like Polat to me."

"This is a mess," Hawk muttered.

Then he heard a creak again. It sounded the same as the last one, only now he knew it was coming from another room.

"I think I've got some hostiles," Hawk whispered. "Just a heads up."

Hawk slipped into the hallway, his head on a swivel and gun trained in front of him.

Another creak. Then he made one of his own.

Footsteps pounded against the floor, beating a path toward the back of the apartment. Hawk switched into pursuit mode, unsure of why whoever else was inside had waited until that moment to attempt a quick exit. Though Hawk had moved stealthily down the hall, it wasn't as if his entrance was unannounced.

A blur darted to the left at the end of the short corridor, and Hawk followed suit. Another blur to the right, only this time, Hawk caught a glimpse of a man clutching something in his left hand.

When Hawk reached the back, the man was trying to unlock the door but was having trouble, the kind that gets a person killed. The man looked over his shoulder at Hawk standing in the doorway and fired several shots. Hawk dashed behind the wall and waited.

Three . . . two . . . one.

Hawk exploded around the corner and squeezed off two shots. The first one hit the man in the shoulder, the second one in his head. He collapsed, dropping both his gun and the small device he'd been holding. It was a flash drive. Hawk kicked the gun away from the man and stooped down to check his pulse. He was dead.

Hawk pocketed the device. "Well, Polat's dead, but at least we got what we came here for," he said into his comlink.

Then another creak.

Hawk looked up to find another man raising his gun when three shots ripped through him and he toppled to the floor. Heavy footfalls followed before Samuels appeared in the doorway. He shook his head.

"Next time, you need to listen to me and follow protocol," Samuels said. "If I hadn't broken protocol myself, you'd be dead right now."

Hawk winked and pulled the flash drive out of his pocket. He held it up for Samuels.

"But we wouldn't have this either, which was the entire point of this mission."

Alex interrupted the conversation. "This tit-for-tat is fun, but you two have a pair of uninvited guests heading up the front stairs now."

Hawk took aim at the lock and fired two shots, shattering it and freeing the door. The two operatives raced outside and headed for their truck.

"What are you going to do now?" Samuels asked as he kept pace with Hawk.

"What? Your little manual doesn't describe how to handle a situation like this?" Hawk fired back, still in a dead sprint.

As they rounded the corner, a shot ricocheted off a nearby building.

Alex met them at the door, holding it up as Hawk and Samuels rushed inside.

"Samuels, drive this thing like you stole it," Hawk said.

"What are you gonna do?" Samuels asked as he turned the key and shifted the van into gear.

"Just drive."

Samuels stomped on the gas. Alex and Hawk both lurched back but they quickly regained their balance.

Hawk looked at Alex and pointed at the front seat. "You don't want to be back here for this, but I'm going to lose them for you."

She shook her head and sighed as she glanced at the motorcycle in the rear of the van. "On that thing?"

"Got any better ideas? Samuels didn't have any from his manual."

"Just make it back alive, will you?"

"I always do," Hawk said, securing the chinstrap on his helmet.

Hawk kicked down on the starter and revved the engine several times. He hit a button on the side of the van and activated the door, rolling it up overhead. The moment the door raised high enough for Hawk to slip beneath, he roared out and hit the street hard. He quickly spun around and accelerated.

Looking over his shoulder, Hawk identified the two men chasing them now speeding toward them in a black SUV. They fired a few bursts at him before Hawk identified a side street to draw them away from the van.

Hawk banked hard left, and the men followed.

"Alex, can you help me out here?" Hawk asked.

"Give me a second," she said. "I'm calling up a map."

Hawk slowed down just enough to take a hard right onto another street.

"Okay, I've got something. In about a quarter of a mile on the right, there's an alley you can lose them in."

"You sure that's a good route?"

"There might be a few steps involved, but I'm sure you can handle it."

Hawk huffed a short laugh through his nose. "You never like to give me the easy way, do you?"

"Where's the fun in that?"

Hawk glanced over his shoulder at the SUV now gaining on him. He weaved again, anticipating the men were close enough to begin firing again. Several more shots whizzed past before Hawk whipped his bike hard right and into the alley Alex picked out for him. He zoomed down the narrow passageway, which wound around to a large plaza. However, in order to get back onto the main road, Hawk had to navigate a series of steps, which sent people scattering as he bounced past.

When he came back to the main road, he checked and discovered the SUV was nowhere to be found.

"Think you can get me back to the warehouse now?" Hawk asked.

"Piece of cake," Alex said before passing along the instructions.

Once Hawk returned, he hustled through the door, pushing his bike inside as well.

"What? No welcoming committee?" Hawk asked with a wink.

"We only throw parties when you actually capture the target, not for just escaping one of her minions," Samuels said.

"Is that part of the manual, too?" Hawk asked.

Samuels took a deep breath and crossed his arms before speaking without a hint of expression. "You're a funny guy, Brady Hawk."

"So I've been told. But this is way more exciting work than standup comedy, though I'm certain it's probably just about as terrifying."

"What? You get scared standing up in front of audiences?" Samuels asked. "Someone who totes his confidence around like it's a trophy wife?"

"I prefer action to speaking," Hawk said. "You can communicate much more clearly and precisely that way."

Sitting at a computer terminal in one corner of the room, Alex cleared her throat in an attempt to put a stop to the banter. "I also prefer action as well," she said, "which is why we need to start looking at this flash drive that cost Ahmet Polat his life."

Hawk and Samuels joined her as she began typing away on the keyboard.

"What are we looking at here?" Hawk asked.

"We're looking at our best shot at taking down Katarina Petrov and The Chamber."

CHAPTER 2

Stuttgart, Germany

KATARINA PETROV LOOSELY HELD a cigarette in her hand and stared out across the city from the rooftop of her temporary penthouse suite. Taking a long drag, she blew a lungful of smoke into the air and turned toward Heinrich Doblestort, the German chancellor who was reluctant to go along with Petrov's latest scheme. He swirled the liquid around in his glass, staring pensively at it.

"Well, aren't you going to say something?" Petrov asked. "No problem was ever solved by staring at a glass of scotch."

Doblestort looked up at Petrov and sighed. He then turned and stared out across the city skyline. "Perhaps, but it does help me forget a few unsavory decisions I've had to make."

"What kind of leadership is that? I thought you

had a backbone," Petrov said, needling Doblestort. "Maybe I should seek help elsewhere."

"No, no," Doblestort said. "Don't do that. I think I can help you. It's just that—"

"Just that what? You don't like being wealthy? You don't like owing someone something? You don't like being on the right side of history because God knows as a German you could use some help in that category."

Doblestort responded with a steely gaze. "I never make decisions hastily. That's how this *good* leader handles problems."

Petrov returned the cigarette to her lips and sucked in another drag. She exhaled a small plume of smoke before saying a word. "Sometimes leaders don't have time to contemplate every angle of their decisions. Sometimes you have to act on instinct. What are your instincts telling you, Heinrich?"

"They're telling me to run," he said flatly. "They're telling me to distance myself from you as much as possible and never look back."

Petrov clucked her tongue. "Heinrich, Heinrich, Heinrich. That would be most unfortunate. I need you to comply or else you'll force me to do unsavory things to you and your loved ones. And honestly, I'd prefer to avoid such unpleasantries. We've been friends for a long time now, and you know I don't issue threats, especially empty ones. I only make promises, the kind of promises I swear to keep. And I can assure you the only promises you want me to keep are the ones that result in you getting rich."

Doblestort glanced back down at his glass. "Fine. I'll do it. I'll help you set up the meeting. But that's as far as it goes with me."

"That's as far as I'll need you to take it," she said. "The rest will be up to me—and I have full confidence in my ability to help everyone see it's in their best interest to cooperate."

"No dirty tactics," Heinrich said.

"Of course not, Heinrich. Don't be silly. I always play by the rules in these types of situations. If I coerce someone against their will, I run the risk of being accused later on. And scurrilous accusations are not something The Chamber looks upon fondly."

Doblestort tilted his head back and downed the remaining scotch in his glass. Looking at Petrov, he said, "Let's go discuss the details then."

On their way across the balcony back inside Petrov's suite, a news report played on the television. The handsome man seated behind the BBC news desk was giving the latest details about an incident in the Middle East.

"In one of the higher profile journalist abductions in recent years, *New York Times* war correspondent Lee Powell was abducted today during a live video report from Afghanistan. He was covering a skirmish outside of Kabul that broke out late yesterday evening. However, when he went to file a live report with the action in the background, a group of terrorists snatched him and drove off, leaving his camera still running. Officials have yet to determine who is responsible for the kidnapping, though more than a half-dozen known terrorist organizations have claimed responsibility. However, one U.S. official from the Pentagon said all indications point toward Al Hasib as the responsible party."

"A bunch of fools still trying to be relevant," Doblestort said, scoffing at the report. "They are so desperate to gain the sort of attention that made ISIS and other groups famous that they resort to guerilla tactics on such an easy, low-value target. They will get nothing from him."

Petrov waved him off. "Crazy world we live in, but I wouldn't dismiss them so quickly. It doesn't take much to make a comeback in today's terroristic environment."

"You would know, wouldn't you?"

She didn't look up, tapping slowly on her phone's screen. After a few seconds, she stopped and proceeded to sit at the table.

As Doblestort joined her, his attention was

arrested by a buzzing phone. He picked it up and glanced at the screen. His eyes widened before he turned his focus toward Petrov.

"Why?" he said, holding up his phone. "Why would you do this? I already said I would help. This isn't right."

"Just making sure everyone marches to the same beat, Heinrich," she said. "We can't have people making their own rhythm if this is going to work."

"I can't believe you would do something like this."

"You can't? A few moments ago you seemed to suggest that I was little more than a terrorist myself."

"I said that in jest, but now I see I was right all along."

Petrov smiled and laughed softly. "Well, you do whatever you like, but if you don't want to embarrass that pretty little wife of yours and those five beautiful children you have, I suggest you put this plan into motion." She slid a file folder across the table at him. "It'd be a pity if those pictures found their way to the internet, catalogued for the world to see for all of eternity."

He grabbed the papers off the table and responded tersely. "I'll get right on this, your highness."

CHAPTER 3

Washington, D.C.

J.D. BLUNT CHEWED ON A CIGAR as he climbed aboard a Segway. The motorized device rolled forward smoothly before Blunt stopped it and spun around to face his entourage. Hawk, Alex, and Samuels stared back at Blunt with slight smirks.

"Would any of you mind telling me what you're laughing at?" Blunt asked.

Alex spoke up first. "Nothing, sir. It's just that—" She stopped, unable to contain her laughter any longer. Hawk and Samuels joined her.

"So, you think it's funny to see an old man on top of one of these machines?" Blunt asked. "I'll have you know that you'll all be wishing you had one of these in a half hour when we're still walking." He zipped the machine around in the opposite direction. "Now, come along."

Blunt powered the machine forward, and with a slight lurch began his journey toward the White House's secret meeting room buried beneath the bowels of Washington.

Just before the Library of Congress was completed in the late 1800s, the famous architect Edward Casey was brought in to oversee the final stages of construction. Casey's father had served as a brigadier general in the the Army Corps of Engineers—and it was at his request that a network of tunnels were constructed between the library and several key government buildings in Washington in case high profile officials ever needed to escape a siege. One of those buildings was the White House.

"What kind of excursion is this?" Hawk asked after following Blunt for nearly a half hour through narrowing tunnels that seemed to darken with every step. "Is this one of your life lessons?"

Blunt chuckled. "I can assure you that I prefer to teach my life lessons on a boat in the open water while holding a glass of scotch. This wouldn't be my preferred way."

"So, this trip has a purpose?" Samuels asked.

Blunt nodded. "Indeed it does."

"I don't remember reading about this in any of the documents you gave me before I joined the team," Samuels said. "I'm getting uncomfortable with this, sir."

"Geez, Samuels. You must be a lot of fun at parties."

"The life of them, sir," Samuels said matter of factly. "It's what seeing the world does for a young man. It gives him a sense of purpose and meaning in life, not to mention some kick ass stories to share around the punch bowl."

"Punch bowl?" Alex asked incredulously. "Blunt, where the hell did you dig this guy up? And why did you place him on our team?"

Blunt gnawed on his cigar for several more seconds before taking it out of his mouth. "I'm going to let someone else explain all of that to you in just a few minutes. Not much farther now."

True to his word, Blunt finally came to a stop and climbed off his Segway in front of what appeared to be a dead end. The narrow tunnel had widened just before it ran out, leaving his companions in a bewildered state.

He smiled and asked, "So, anyone want to make fun of my wheels now?"

All three were quiet.

"I didn't think so."

Alex spoke up. "So, this was one of your lessons? Just drag us through a bunch of tunnels and wear us down while you simply roll along on your little Segway. I'm not sure what the lesson is here, sir, but it certainly seems like a cruel one."

Blunt crammed his cigar back into his mouth. "Oh, I'm sorry, Alex. Were you under the impression that we had arrived at our final destination? I'm afraid we still have to walk a little bit more."

He walked toward the wall and put his hand on it. Seconds later, a panel slid open, revealing a dashboard of electronics. Blunt leaned in and opened his eyes wide.

"Oh, a retinal scan," Alex said. "Standard in most Washington tunnels from what I hear."

Blunt watched the doors in front of him open. "More than you know, Alex."

He strode ahead, glancing back at the trio to make sure they were following. The new section of the tunnel was state of the art, clean, and flanked by small rooms off to the side.

"What is this place?" Samuels asked.

"It's where they make the manuals," Hawk deadpanned. "But you better not touch anything, per item T, section three on page forty-seven."

"Ha ha," Samuels said. "Real funny, Hawk."

"Oh, so he does understand sarcasm," Alex said as a wry grin spread across her face.

"This way," Blunt said, directing them toward an elevator. Once they were all inside, he swiped a card in front of a black pad. A muted ding came from the overhead speaker, and the elevator descended.

Blunt enjoyed the looks on their faces, confident

they would all expect to go up.

"How deep does this thing go?" Samuels asked.

Blunt smiled. "Deep enough."

After about half a minute, the door slid open and Blunt led them into another corridor before turning the corner. He walked up to a door, which was guarded by a pair of secret servicemen. One of the men opened the door and held it as he motioned for Blunt and his entourage to enter.

"The president has been expecting you," he said.

Blunt hobbled toward a sitting area with three small couches and two chairs. He walked up to President Noah Young, who stood to welcome his guests, and shook hands.

"J.D., I'm so glad your team could join me here today," Young said. "Can I offer any one of you a drink?"

"They definitely need hydration after that walk," Blunt said with a chuckle. "They complained so much I think I know how Moses felt leading the Israelites out of Egypt."

"As long as there were no marauding Egyptians hot in pursuit, I think it's probably safe to proceed," Young cracked.

"None on the radar, sir," Hawk said. "We do our best to make sure we cover our tracks so nobody can follow us."

"Very well then," Young said, clapping his hands

and rubbing them together. "Let's proceed. Please, have a seat."

Young sat down first and leaned forward in his chair, while the rest of the Firestorm team followed his instructions.

"Now, J.D. tells me you have some important information for me, but before we get to that, I thought I would formally introduce you to the newest team member I requested to be placed with you."

Young gestured toward Samuels.

"Shane Samuels was placed in your unit at my special request for a number of reasons," Young said. "For starters, I needed to have a way to connect with your team if Michaels somehow manages to regain control of the presidency. At this point, I think it's a long shot, but you never can be too sure in Washington. Nothing is a given, and I mean nothing. Michaels doesn't know about Shane Samuels, and I intend to keep it that way."

"Thank you, sir," Samuels said.

Young continued. "Now, I've known Shane and his family for years and helped him get into the FBI years ago. He worked on a counterintelligence team for the FBI in several countries throughout the Middle East. He's well connected in both official and unofficial capacities. But if anyone tries to find a connection between me and this Firestorm team, they'll be hard pressed to do so, especially now. From now on, all my communication with the team will go through Shane. And it's simply for your protection and for mine in case the unthinkable happens."

"So, once Michaels is removed for good, we can return to normal business operating procedures?" Alex asked.

Young shrugged. "We'll have to play it by ear. Michaels will still have plenty of allies even if he ends up getting tossed out of office. But I hope that will be the case. So, any more questions?"

Nobody said a word. "Excellent. There's one more order of business we need to discuss before moving forward."

"And what exactly is that?" Hawk asked.

"It's about your newest team member."

Samuels shifted uncomfortably in his seat. Young's connection to him already appeared to make him uncomfortable, but with the acting president's latest comment, the newest Firestorm member turned a dark shade of red."

"What about him?" Alex asked. "He's certainly a dedicated rule follower."

Young placed his hands on his knees and leaned back before taking in a deep breath. "That's not all he is."

"What do you mean?" Blunt asked.

Young surveyed his audience for a moment and

then proceeded. "He's also Alex's brother."

Alex's mouth fell agape. "My brother? But I—"

"Half brother to be more precise. Your father had an affair with an FBI agent about five years after you were born, Alex. It was kept quiet for a number of reasons, reasons which the bureau was content to oblige him with. I knew his mother from several interagency collaborative projects I worked on and eventually became good friends with her and her husband."

"This is strange," she said. "I'm not sure how I feel about all of this."

"I'm not asking you to feel any way about it," Young said. "All I'm asking you to do is to work together and get along. Think you can do that?"

She nodded slowly.

"You good with that Hawk?"

Hawk shrugged. "I guess so. You might want to ask Samuels if it's in the manual because he seems to have a difficult time proceeding without knowing where it's located within the book."

Samuels shot Hawk a nasty look.

"Sometimes you just have to go off book," Young said.

"Thank you," Hawk said, looking at Samuels while gesturing toward the president. "See, I've been telling you that, but you won't listen. We don't have to follow everything in the manual just because it's there."

Young cleared his throat and eyed Hawk closely. "But we don't need to discard it altogether. The manual is there for a purpose—and usually that purpose is to protect us. Understand?"

Hawk nodded. "Understood, sir."

"Good," Young said as he snapped. "Now, let's get down to the real reason we came here. I understand that you have something to show us, Alex."

Alex dug into her pocket for the flash drive and held it out. "Do you have a computer for me to work on, Mr. President?"

"Of course I do." He stood and retrieved a laptop from a desk in the corner of the room. "Will this work?"

She nodded. "It should do the trick."

Slipping the flash drive into the USB port on the computer, she waited a moment for the folder to appear on the desktop.

"Where did this information come from?" Young asked.

"A counterintelligence asset by the name of Ahmet Polat. He'd been gathering intelligence on The Chamber, and more specifically Katarina Petrov, our favorite traitor and murderer of a mother."

"Have you been to therapy for that?" Samuels asked. "Because I know a really good—"

"I'd stop right there if I were you," Hawk

warned. "You know that part a few seconds ago where she mentioned she prefers action?"

Hawk let the implication of his question sink in for a moment, a clue that Samuels quickly got and heeded. He remained quiet while Alex worked.

"Look at this file," Alex said.

"Scheduled meetings," Hawk read. "This has some interesting information inside."

Alex clicked on a file folder. Immediately, a document opened that listed all of The Chamber's meetings, including several names of famous leaders within the global financial sector who Hawk recognized.

"Do you know how all these people are connected to The Chamber?" Alex asked.

"We're not sure how in bed they are with her," Hawk said. "They could just be ancillary partners, knowingly or not. Petrov has incredible sway on people."

Alex nodded. "And if she can't persuade them with her words, she sure knows how to leverage people's secrets against them."

"Whatever she's up to, there's only one meeting on here that looks worth crashing," Hawk said as he tapped a specific line on the monitor.

Young exhaled and patted Samuels on the back. "Looks like the Firestorm team has its next new mission. Wheels up in twelve hours. You're heading to Stuttgart."

CHAPTER 4

Stuttgart, Germany

PETROV TOOK THE TABLET from her aide, Anatoly, and stared at the screen. She studied the numbers closely, grimacing at some, expressing delight at others. After several minutes, she set the device on the table and sighed.

"I know it's not what we were hoping for, but it's a start," Anatoly said.

Petrov waved him off. "I'm not sure the others will see it that way. We're not playing the market here; we're trying to wreak havoc with it."

She stood and paced around the room for several minutes, fingers steepled and pressed to her lips.

"Would you care for a drink?" Anatoly asked, breaking the silence.

She shook her head as she paced. "We will never hit our target if we don't become more aggressive."

"I agree, but being aggressive in our current financial environment requires some stealth. We are supposed to operate behind the curtain, if I recall correctly."

Petrov meandered toward the balcony, pausing briefly to slide open the glass door. She walked outside and pulled out a cigarette, holding it to her lips. Anatoly flicked his lighter and offered the flame to her. She stooped slightly and sucked in, the tobacco crackling as it caught fire.

"We only need to be shrouded as long as it takes to send the market in turmoil," she said. "If the two things happen at once, it won't matter."

Anatoly shrugged. "If you think that's best, please proceed. Tomorrow's meeting could be most uncomfortable if you're unable to explain where we go from here."

"The Chamber answers to no one," she said, casting a sideways glance at her aide. "Besides, those in attendance at tomorrow's meeting won't utter a single complaint if all goes according to plan."

"How exactly do you intend to appease them?"

"It will be subtle yet effective. In the meantime, we have to do more to shake these markets up."

Anatoly folded his arms and eyed her closely. "So, do you have any ideas on how to do that?"

She shrugged. "Perhaps I do. However, it will be

bold and brazen."

"Just like you, no?"

Petrov smiled. "You need to work on your flattery. It isn't so subtle if I can see right through it." She took a long drag on her cigarette. "I do love a good compliment though."

"I just meant—"

"Sshhh," Petrov said, holding up her index finger. "Any attempts to explain yourself will only make it worse. What I need right now are ideas on how to bring more instability to the market, preferably before next week's gathering with the board."

"You're satisfied that the German financial leaders will follow your lead at the meeting tomorrow?"

"I'm not so concerned about them. We have more powerful people who must be satisfied."

Anatoly gestured toward Petrov's cigarette. "May I?"

She handed it to him and watched him suck in a long breath before exhaling.

"There is someone who might be able to assist you," Anatoly said.

She turned her gaze toward him. "I'm listening."

"Before this person will agree to anything, you'll need to meet with him in person."

"If he's capable of doing what needs to be done, I'll travel anywhere."

"That's a good thing because you just might have to. He's not exactly the kind of person who comes to you."

Petrov retrieved her cigarette from Anatoly. "I'm satisfied going anywhere if the end result means the market is turned on its head so The Chamber can accomplish its goals."

"I can almost guarantee you he'll be able to accomplish that for you."

"Excellent," she said. "Set up a meeting, and I'll be there."

CHAPTER 5

Stuttgart, Germany

HAWK WINKED HIS LEFT EYE as he stared through the telescopic lens at the building adjacent to his position. He growled once he noticed the blinds remained closed. Other than his inability to see into the actual room, everything else was going as planned.

"How's that hack of the security feed coming along, Alex?" Hawk asked.

"Not there yet, but I'm close."

"We need it pronto," he said. "Everyone is expected to be in the room in a matter of minutes."

"And, of course, we need to get confirmation that all the people inside are who they're purported to be," Samuels said. "Without that, we can't fire the first shot."

Hawk sighed and shook his head. "Samuels, when you go home at night, do you stay up late memorizing portions of the manual? Curious minds want to know."

"I know you're mocking me right now," Samuels said. "Just because I'm well-versed on the ways of protocol doesn't mean I have no life."

"Is that so?" Hawk asked. "Who's your favorite band?"

Samuels furrowed his brow. "Don't you mean *composer*?"

Hawk threw his hands in the air. "I give up. Alex, he's your brother."

"*Half* brother," she said sternly.

"Pardon me if I'm not up on the latest pop culture craze taking America by storm," Samuels said. "That isn't my job. I'm paid to help keep this country safe by rooting out threats. That's my job—and that's what I'm good at."

Hawk buried his head in his hands before glancing up at Samuels. "Well, Mr. I'm-Good-at-My-Job, do you think you can help me out and see through the blinds in this room across the way or help Alex hack the security feed in the building next door? We're running out of time, and there's nothing more I hate than being unprepared."

"Now you're speaking my language," Samuels said as he leaned forward and pressed his face to the telescope. "I'm always prepared."

"What do you see?" Hawk asked.

"I'm good at gathering information that isn't supposed to be leaked. That's a far cry from the ability to see through window blinds."

Hawk rubbed his forehead. "Still closed?"

"I'm afraid so," Samuels said as he backed away from the lens.

"Maybe you can give me a hand," Alex said. "I can't seem to find an override on this security system."

"Sibling cooperation—it warms my heart," Hawk said as he cracked a smile.

"You do realize there are two of us and only one of you, right?" Alex said.

"I think I could take both of you."

"Don't be so modest," Samuels said as he sat down in front of Alex's computer. "You'd think you could take three or four of us if there were that many."

Hawk shook his head. "We haven't even completed two missions together and you already know me so well, Samuels. You're going to fit right in on this team."

"Well, *this team* is going to find itself in a heap of trouble if we can't get eyes inside that room," Alex said as she pointed at the building across the street. "Blunt and the president—"

"Acting president," Samuels interjected.

Alex gave him a sideways glance before continuing. "Blunt and the *acting president* are counting on us to deliver, and we can't let them down."

"Aside from X-ray vision, what do you suggest?" Hawk asked.

"I need to physically go to the building to gain access to the mainframe," Alex said. "They've got a damn good firewall, which I could hack, but not in time."

"I'll do it," Samuels said.

"Oh, Samuels," Hawk said with a dismissive wave. "Don't bother yourself with it. I'll hustle over there to get it done for Alex."

"No, no. Please allow me," Samuels responded. "I've seen your marksmanship scores. You're a better shot than I am."

Hawk eyed him cautiously. "I was hoping you could help me shoot."

"I'll make it quick," Samuels said before he hustled out of the room and exited the apartment space they'd rented for the assignment.

"I'm quickly learning that you can't tell him anything," Alex said.

"Guess it runs in the family genes," Hawk said as he leaned back into the telescopic lens.

"Anything?"

"The blinds are all still pulled. And quite frankly,

I'm starting to get a little nervous about this."

"Ditto for me," Alex said. "What's weird is the fact that from everything I can see, the security feed is functioning. It's almost as if *they* took it down for some reason."

"Software update?"

"That was how I initially planned to get into the system. That's why it's going to take much more now."

"I'm hoping things move more quickly once Samuels gets you online and someone opens those damn blinds," Hawk said. "Who knows how long before we get another shot like this."

Ten minutes later, Samuels hailed Hawk and Alex on the coms. "Okay, guys. I'm in."

"Already?" Alex asked, mouth agape.

"The acting president didn't assign me to this team because of my winsome good looks," Samuels said.

Hawk chuckled. "No, he certainly didn't."

Alex typed furiously for the next minute until she threw her hands in the air and made the announcement Samuels and Hawk were waiting to hear.

"I'm in," she said.

"On my way back now," Samuels said.

Hawk walked across the room and stooped behind Alex, studying her screen over her shoulder.

"Are you running facial recognition?"

"Just started it, but I know from our files that those two right there were in the dossier Blunt left us on the plane," she said as she pointed at the monitor.

"Are you sure?" Hawk asked.

"Positive."

The image on the screen flashed before everything came back into focus.

Hawk squinted. "What was that?"

"I think it was the camera adjusting to the light."

Hawk rushed back over to the window and looked through the lens again. "The blinds are open."

He didn't waste any time in running through a rapid checklist for his sniper rifle. Taking out another box of ammunition, he sighted in his weapon.

"Think you're going to need all of that?" Alex asked, gesturing toward the bullets. "There are only six of them in the room."

"I'm saving those for Petrov."

Alex sighed. "It's a strange feeling to hear you say that about my mother, yet I'm in complete agreement with you. She needs to be taken down, and I'd rather you do it than anyone else."

Samuels burst into the room, slamming the door behind him. "Have we verified everyone's identities yet?"

Alex's computer beeped. "We've verified one."

"That program needs to speed up," Samuels said. "According to the schedule we took off Polat's flash drive, the meeting is only supposed to last ten more minutes."

Hawk grunted. "You ever been in one of those meetings? They always last longer than you think."

Alex's machine beeped two more times, then a third. "Just waiting on confirmation of two more faces. But so far, so good."

The seconds ticked past, far too quickly for Hawk's taste. "Alex, talk to me. We need to make a move soon. We're going to miss our chance if they all get up and exit the room. And that could happen at any minute."

"I can't make the program work any faster," she said. "It's not like I can tap into a bigger processer from this location."

"And we're not firing a shot until we receive confirmation on the identities of everyone in the room," Samuels said.

"Of course, you have to bring up protocol, don't you?" Hawk said.

"Without protocol, what do we have? Chaos? Pandemonium?"

"Perhaps we'll have an entire room of The Chamber's dead board members," Hawk said. "But we may never know, will we?"

"Sorry, guys," Alex said. "I'm doing all I can."

Just as she finished speaking, her computer beeped.

"Is that a go?" Hawk asked.

"Our sixth and final confirmation, right there," she said.

"We're up, Samuels," Hawk said as he placed his right eye up against his scope. "Wait a minute. What's going on?"

"They're all getting up, like the meeting is over," Samuels said.

"Alex, can you get audio from the feed?" Hawk asked.

"This is a video-only system," she said.

"Yeah and we're too far away for my directional mic to pick up anything."

"Hold on," Samuels said. "They're sitting back down—and they don't look too happy about it from what I can tell. Petrov is directing them all back to the table."

"When did Petrov come into the room?" Alex asked. "She wasn't in there earlier."

"Just a second ago as they were all about to leave," Samuels said.

"Save Petrov for me, Samuels," Hawk said. "She's mine."

"Suit yourself."

The two operatives took their positions and methodically picked off board members seated around the table. Hawk took the left side, Samuels the right. In a matter of seconds, they were all dead, except for Petrov.

She raced toward the door but struggled to get it open.

"What's she doing?" Samuels asked.

Hawk squeezed off two rounds, the first one ripped through the back of her head. The second one tore into her back left shoulder blade. She collapsed to the ground. Hawk took a moment to study the scene. The clean shots happened too quickly; the first few people likely never knew what hit them while the last couple of people never had a chance to react. Only Petrov was left to squirm in her final seconds before Hawk ended her life.

"That's a wrap," Hawk said. "Let's get the hell outta here before we attract any attention."

* * *

HAWK WAITED UNTIL THEY were in the air before placing a call to Blunt. Satisfied with how the operation went down, Hawk was confident his superior would be pleased with the results.

"Have you heard the good news?" Hawk asked. "The Chamber board has been eliminated."

"Are you sure about that?" Blunt asked. "Because

that's not the way I understand it."

Hawk furrowed his brow. "What are you talking about?"

"There's a report blowing up the networks right now about a brazen attack that killed seven heads of the German banking industry, an attack that sounded vaguely familiar to the one you were planning."

"Sounds like a strange coincidence to me."

Blunt took a deep breath. "Weren't you shooting at the Byzantine Office Building?"

"That's the one."

"It's a damn strange coincidence, then, because that's the same building all these bankers were in. And what's even stranger is that security footage being played all over television shows three suspects who look a lot like the three of you."

"That's impossible," Hawk said. "We used facial recognition to verify their identities before shooting. We followed protocol."

"For once," Blunt said.

"You gotta believe me. We wouldn't proceed unless we knew the targets were verified. You know me well enough to know I wouldn't do that."

"I also know you well enough to understand that you hate Katarina Petrov with a passion and have it out for her personally. If you even thought you had a chance to take her down, I doubt you would've waited to follow protocol before pulling that trigger."

"So that wasn't her?"

"The woman who was murdered was Madeline Schumer, head of Frankfurt International Bank."

"No way. I swear that was Petrov. Alex confirmed it before we started shooting."

"I'm inclined to believe you, Hawk, but that doesn't change the fact that you're now fugitives and the U.S. government can't do a damn thing to help you."

"Come on," Hawk said. "You've gotta help us. If everyone from the FBI to Interpol is chasing us, we don't stand a chance."

"I'm sure you'll find a way," Blunt said. "Just make sure you stay out of sight once you get back here, and stay in touch. You might still be able to help us."

"Petrov set us up," Hawk mumbled to himself as he hung up the phone.

CHAPTER 6

Tangier, Morocco

KATARINA PETROV GRINNED as she scrolled through the news article on her phone about the brazen attack on the heads of the German finance industry. Stocks sank as the report shook the confidence many investors had in the European market. The direction German investing was headed brought certainty to the market, but that was no longer the case. Analysts and pundits alike voiced their fears about what might become. Nothing seemed certain, except more uncertainty.

Petrov put down her phone and lit a cigarette. She glanced out across the water before closing her eyes and putting her face to the sun.

"It's a beautiful day," a man said, interrupting her blissful moment.

She looked up to see her appointment had

arrived and gave him a wry smile. "Well, that depends." She gestured for him to sit down across the table.

"On what?" he asked as he pulled his chair out and took a seat.

"On what you can do for me, Karif. I had a beautiful day yesterday, but if our meeting goes well, perhaps this will be one too."

Karif Fazil leaned back in his chair, crossed his legs, and clasped his hands, resting them on his knee. "I understand you require some assistance, though I'm not sure it's the kind of thing we operate in any more. But before we discuss that, I'm curious how you set up the American assassin and his team."

She took a long drag before exhaling. "Simple parlor tricks. Making the mind see what it wants to see is the kind of wizardry that's been around for centuries. It only takes a little bit more effort these days with facial recognition cameras, but they're susceptible too."

"Who did he think he was shooting?" Fazil asked.

"Certainly not the reported names of the ones who ended up dead. But that's not why we're here now, is it?"

"Forgive my indulgence, Katarina, but you must understand that I have both a high level of respect for

Brady Hawk *and* a powerful disdain for him. If it weren't for Hawk's meddling in my affairs, I'm sure the mission of Al Hasib would be far more advanced."

"In that case, let's talk about how I can help you move your cause forward now that Hawk has more or less been eliminated from the picture."

"And how do you think you can help us do that?"

"The one thing almost as old as my parlor tricks: money."

"So this is about money then?"

Petrov tapped the ashes off her cigarette. "You require funds to operate, do you not?"

Fazil nodded. "Of course. Who doesn't? But you want us to strike the pipelines?"

"That's the plan."

"The same pipelines that provide us with our current level of funding. That would be—how do they say it in America?—cutting off the nose to spite the face. I'm not sure that's something we can afford."

"Those pipelines provide you with a small trickle of income," Petrov said. "I think you'd prefer something more substantial, something that would amount to a gushing river of cash."

"I'm listening."

"If you stick with me, I think we can have a fruitful partnership, enabling you to advance the noble mission of Al Hasib."

Fazil eyed her cautiously. "And Al Hasib's mission is likely in direct conflict with yours."

"Not necessarily," she said, sucking in another long drag before blowing smoke upward out of the corner of her mouth. "From what I can tell, you and I are both visionaries, people who want to shake up the status quo. We're tired of the world being run by a small, elite group of people who have little regard for those who aren't like themselves." She paused. "Does any of this ring true with you?"

He nodded. "Go on."

"Even your own people betray you and your cause—and that includes those running the pipelines in Kuwait City. Those people need to understand they can't run over you or me or anyone else, just like the Americans need to be taught the same message. Liberty and justice for all? In their dreams. It's all about wealth and prosperity for U.S. citizens and no one else. And if you help me, we can end two suffocating regimes making it difficult for our own dreams to be realized at once."

Fazil exhaled and locked eyes with Petrov. "I hope you're not lying to me, because I don't appreciate it when people try to woo me with their persuasive tongues."

"I would never lie to such an honorable man as yourself, Karif," she said.

"Very well then."

"So, we have a deal?"

Petrov smiled and nodded. "I'll forward you all the schematics of the compound and pipeline I want you to attack. It shouldn't be too difficult for you given your history."

* * *

NEITHER PETROV NOR FAZIL noticed the man reading a newspaper two tables away. He never stopped watching Petrov, who never made eye contact with him. He was invisible, just the way he liked it. It was beneficial to his climb up the bureau's ladder. Getting made by a pair of well-known terrorists was no way to advance one's career, much less survive.

He waited until the duo vacated their table before asking for his check. Once he paid his bill, he promptly returned to his hotel room, where he uploaded several pictures he casually snapped with his phone and sent them to his director. Within an hour, the FBI was liaising with the Pentagon regarding the formation of a new threat.

Commander Frank Stone received the message and took his new assignment seriously. He knew all about Karif Fazil and Katarina Petrov and despised both of them. Stone wished he'd been the one present for their meeting, relishing the opportunity to take them out in one fell swoop.

"Sir," one of Stone's aides began, "how do you think we should proceed with this, given the fact we aren't authorized to take any action on foreign soil until this whole issue with President Michaels gets settled?"

"Are you sure we can't find an angle that shows this is a direct threat to us here in America?"

"Not unless you want to go to prison," the aide answered. "I already broached the subject with the DOJ with a hypothetical situation. They said no dice."

"Very well then. I know someone who might be able to help us."

"Who's that?"

"It's an old friend," Stone said. "And I'm sure he'll know a way we can handle it."

CHAPTER 7

Washington, D.C.

HAWK LOOKED OUT HIS WINDOW and watched the U.S. coastline come into view. Despite all of America's foibles, Hawk couldn't think of a better place in the world to live. The land of opportunity still thrived with people imagining a better life, even if it was little more than a pipedream. There was something about citizens having collective hope that gave a country energy. And in his world travels, Hawk hadn't felt anything close to what he experienced in the U.S.

"Beautiful view, isn't it?" Alex asked, snapping Hawk out of his trance.

"Yeah, the shoreline is always a sight to behold from the air."

"Are you okay?" she asked as she slipped into the seat adjacent Hawk.

"Yeah, I guess so. I'm a little disappointed Petrov duped us like she did and I'm responsible for killing innocent people, but other than that—"

"That wasn't your fault, Hawk. We did everything by the book. There's no way we could've known."

"But we should have. We're better than that. There were some clues something just wasn't right—and we glossed right over them. *I* glossed right over them. I wanted to take Petrov out so bad that I let it cloud my judgment."

"We're not perfect. We make mistakes."

"Mistakes are not using a big enough caliber bullet for the job, not killing innocent people."

Alex put her hand on Hawk's knee and grabbed his hand. "Don't beat yourself up over this. We all played a part in what went down in Stuttgart. You're not alone here."

"That's not how I operate, Alex. You ought to know that by now. When this team bears responsibility, I have to bear it all. I don't know any other way."

"Well, take your mind off that for a while. You're not going to solve anything by worrying about it."

Hawk shrugged. "Maybe not, but it might make me more vigilant in the future so something like this doesn't happen again—if we ever get a chance to work again."

"We'll figure a way out of this. We always do."

Hawk rubbed his face with both hands and looked wide-eyed at Alex. "Do you have any ideas on how to do that?"

"No, but I do have an idea on how to get your mind off of this."

A grin spread across his face. "With Samuels onboard?"

Alex hit Hawk playfully. "In your dreams."

"So, what is this other *less effective* way to get my mind off the manhunt being conducted for us?"

"An ice breaker question."

"Really? An ice breaker? Aren't we past that part in our relationship where we ask each other if the toilet paper rolls off the top or the bottom?"

She chuckled. "That's a pointless discussion because everybody knows it rolls off the bottom. It makes it easier to tear off, in my opinion."

Hawk glared at her. "I'm not sure we're compatible."

"Okay, never mind I said that. The ice breaker question I had for you was about Bollywood. I'm curious how you became such a big fan of Bollywood movies."

Hawk sighed. "What's a kid to do while stuck in Bombay during a sweltering Indian summer except stay indoors and watch Bollywood movies on television."

"Okay, perfect. This is exactly why I asked this question. I never knew you went to India as a child. How'd that happen?"

"My mom was a nurse, burned out and depressed from slaving away in an ER. Same old stuff, same repeat patients. Nothing ever changed. So, she got the bright idea that one summer she would apply to work for this medical agency that placed medical professionals around the world for short terms. Three months was the shortest amount of time they offered, and my mom jumped on it. They had a daycare place that was supposed to be all amazing and wonderful, but it was really just a few ladies who barely spoke English making sure that we got fed every few hours and that the television was working. My mom had much more fun than I did."

"Did you tell her the daycare wasn't as promised?"

"I didn't have the heart," Hawk said. "I could see how much joy it brought her, and I didn't want to squash her spirit. She would've bailed on the program in a heartbeat if I'd told her, even though she was contractually bound to stay the full three months."

Alex shook her head. "Always gotta be the sacrificial hero, don't you?"

"To be honest, it sucked at first, but after a while, I didn't mind it as much. Besides, I found a channel that played primarily Zeenat Aman movies almost every day. Watching her made it all bearable. I was in love."

"How old were you when all this happened?"

"Thirteen."

"Sounds like it turned out to be a fun experience for you."

Hawk sighed and looked down. "It wasn't all fun and games. In fact, it was really difficult at times. That's the summer I learned just how cruel of a place the world can be."

"Why? What happened?"

"One day when no Zeenat Aman movie was on, I stepped outside with one of my friends to eat a popsicle and saw this kid getting dragged through the street by this man. The boy couldn't have been any older than ten, and he was completely powerless to stop the man. Despite his pleas to stop, the man just kept on lumbering along until he stopped in the middle of the road just a few meters past the house where we were staying."

"What did the boy do?"

"I don't know. All I remember was that he was a mean kid, always teasing younger kids. And he was getting a dose of his own medicine."

"Sounds like he deserved it."

Hawk shrugged. "Maybe, but I don't think he'd

done anything to deserve the kind of abuse he endured. There was a pack of older boys following the man and the kid. Once the man released the kid, he stood up to notice he was surrounded by a sneering mob. The other kids were spitting at him and yelling things at him. I asked my friend what they were saying, and he said they were calling him a rat and a liar. The next thing I know, the kids who'd surrounded the boy picked up nearby rocks and hurled them at him. I can still hear his cries echoing in my ears today."

"So you just sat there and watched it all go down?"

"Absolutely not. I couldn't stand for it. I handed my popsicle to my friend and rushed toward the boy, despite my friend pleading for me to come back. He didn't make a very persuasive argument, but he couldn't have stopped me even if he wanted to. I was going to save that boy."

"What happened after that?"

Using his index finger, Hawk pointed at a scar on the left portion of his forehead. "This is what happened. They started throwing rocks at me, which was exactly what I wanted—along with the last thing I wanted. I was hoping to draw their attention away from the boy so I could get him to safety, but I didn't realize how quickly I would become a target."

Alex shook her head. "Well, what did you expect?

You took away the person they decided to villainize. Everybody always needs a good villain."

"This story had more than its fair share of villains. Once I was able to get the boy to the side away from the circle, I felt a strong tug on my collar, pulling me back toward the boys. I craned my neck to turn and see who it was—and it was the man. He just looked at me and scowled before telling me something to the effect that I needed to mind my own business. I wasn't completely proficient in Hindi at the time, but I understood enough."

"What happened to the boy?"

"They dragged him back into the circle and threw more rocks at him."

Samuels, who'd taken the seat in front of Hawk, jumped into the conversation. "Did you try to find a police officer? I would've reported him to the authorities."

"That's the thing. The man who was dragging him down the street was a policeman. It was one of the most shameful things I ever witnessed." Hawk took a deep breath before continuing. "And when they finally stopped throwing stones at the kid, everyone dispersed. A couple of men hustled in and carried the kid away."

Alex squeezed Hawk's hand. "I don't know how you could stand to watch that."

"I couldn't. It was grotesque. Though I've tried

many times, I can't wipe those images from my mind. Those cries, those screams—they stick with you. It might have been just a fun little exercise for those boys chucking rocks at a helpless kid, but it traumatized him. I'm sure a day doesn't go by where he doesn't still think about it, if he's even still alive. I do wish I could've done more, but I was just a scared outsider."

"At least you tried something," Alex said. "I don't know what I would've done had I been in that situation, though you hardly ever see anything like that when you grow up virtually alone out in the country."

The trio was all so engrossed in the conversation that they barely noticed the tires touching down as the plane landed.

"Never again though," Hawk said. "I swore I'd never abandon someone like that again, no matter what."

They all stood and collected their gear. Just as they were about to step off the private jet, Blunt called Hawk.

"What is it?" Hawk asked.

"There is an all-out manhunt for the three of you," Blunt said. "You need to lay low."

"How the hell are we supposed to get out of the airport? If they're searching for us as actively as you're suggesting, this isn't a good place for us to be. There's going to be an inspection."

"I know. It won't be easy, but I'm sure you'll think of something. In the meantime, stay in touch. I might have another assignment for the three of you."

"Really? You want us to stay low to avoid detection, but then you want us to be ready to get back out there? I think you need to consider our well-being and future more before whipping us back and forth on your whims."

"Now look, Hawk. Don't question whether I've got your best in mind when I'm asking you to do these things. If I thought it would put you in danger—or if it wasn't absolutely necessary for *you* to handle a situation—I wouldn't consider it. The last thing I want is you in custody, believe me."

"I believe you, but it's getting more difficult with these directives that are pushing and pulling us in multiple directions. So, which is it going to be? Because it'd probably be easier for us to refuel and jump back on the plane."

"Lay low for now at the new safe house," Blunt said. "I'll be in touch."

Hawk hung up and let out a string of expletives underneath his breath.

"I know that face," Alex said. "What does Blunt want us to do now?"

"Nothing for now, but he did want to let us know that every law enforcement agency in America is searching for us."

"Wonderful," Alex said.

"Why don't we just turn ourselves in and straighten out this whole little misunderstanding?" Samuels chimed in.

"You," Hawk said, pointing at Samuels. "Be quiet. Forget your stupid manual, and listen to me. It's the only way the three of us are going to stay alive and avoid prison. In the meantime, I think I know a way to get us out of here. Stay right here."

Hawk hustled across the hangar and returned five minutes later carrying a bag stuffed full of clothes.

"Here," he said, "put on these uniforms."

Samuels held up one of the blue outfits. "This is what United flight attendants have to wear?"

Hawk nodded. "It's not a fashion statement. It's simply a way out of here, understand?"

The trio quickly put on the attire and caught a ride to the checkpoint on a golf cart. Riding in silence, Hawk contemplated how he would react if the guard at the gate gave them any trouble. He considered slipping behind the man and putting him in a sleep hold, though he wasn't sure that would sufficiently keep the man out long enough to build a sufficient head start to disappear. With every stretch of road around Washington under surveillance, shaking a tail wouldn't be a simple exercise. But it would be a necessary one. And Hawk needed all the time he could buy if it came to that.

Once the golf cart came to a halt, the three dismounted and thanked the driver. He nodded and drove off.

"Follow my lead," Hawk said. "Do just what I do."

He approached the gate and was met at a kiosk by a security guard.

"Afternoon, officer," Hawk said.

The man eyed Hawk closely. "Just where exactly do you think you're going?"

Hawk froze and clenched his fists.

CHAPTER 8

Kabul, Afghanistan

KARIF FAZIL ENJOYED the feeling of being born again. The burden of being the target of every western country's terrorist hunt had weighed on him. But the time away to reinvent himself had been necessary, not only to tweak his appearance in an effort to avoid facial recognition software, but also to regain his sanity. Wreaking havoc on the free world wasn't for the fainthearted, but even the most battle-tested rebel needed to rest and regroup.

If he was honest, he planned on remaining hidden far longer. The more time and distance between his death and becoming active again, the better. Eventually, he'd be forgotten. And when intelligence agencies spotted him, they'd be scrambling to figure out who he was and how he'd ascended into power without anyone knowing about him. At least, that was Fazil's assumption.

They'll never see me coming.

To assume that suddenly the agencies fighting terrorism abroad would be able to track down any of his six hideouts, much less one of them, seemed absurd at best. Fazil moved around randomly, relying on the roll of a dice to determine when and where he'd go next. It was the one way he'd managed to keep his movements disguised as even he never knew where he'd migrate to next until his fate was revealed on a dotted cube.

Petrov's offer had been enough to lure him—and the rest of Al Hasib—out of dormancy. Funding had always been a problem and had become even more so since certain banks started joining in the battle against terrorism. Freezing assets became a quick way to neuter several groups, a tactic Fazil equally admired and despised. Eliminating funds was resourceful and cowardly. Instead of fighting like men, the western forces cowered behind their gods of dollars and euros. To Fazil, it seemed fitting enough since that was what westerners worshipped anyway. He'd observed how they didn't have the sense of community found in the Middle East, the kind necessary to wage war against an enemy more powerful than yourself. Fazil always understood that winning according to his terms was highly unlikely, yet he knew it was a fight that no one he knew would walk away from. Al Hasib was a tight operation, one that possessed the camaraderie among its men to move forward even when the outcome appeared dark.

Fazil felt new life being breathed into Al Hasib. He knelt on his sajj- da and recited the Asr prayer. He preferred to worship in a mosque but had grown accustomed to more private prayers while trying to remain hidden from groups who desired to claim his head as a bounty. When he was finished, he stood and took a deep breath.

Allah, please show me the way.

Fazil didn't sit and wait for an answer. He trusted the next steps would be revealed as he pondered the assignment given to him.

Petrov's request had been simple: destroy Verge Oil Corporation's facility just outside Kuwait City. The pipeline there served much of the region and generated the lion's share of the country's wealth. More than that, it was a source of pride for most Kuwaitis. They boasted about the fact that their dinar was the strongest against the U.S. dollar of any currency in the world. But it had little to do with their ingenuity or special skills; rather, it had everything to do with location. Like a farmer who strikes it rich when he sells hundreds of acres of his land after a burgeoning city surrounds and encroaches upon him,

Kuwait and its people's wealth was little more than the product of good fortune and good timing. But to hear Kuwaitis discuss it, one would've thought they were responsible for creating a recipe for making oil. All of these sentiments helped Fazil channel his focus into taking down Kuwait's wealth in the slyest of ways. He'd never forgiven them for the way they leaned on the U.S. to assist when Saddam Hussein aggressively attacked their oil fields and sought to claim them as his own.

Cowards, every last one of them.

Fazil determined this attack would be a memorable one. If he was going to return Al Hasib to the front pages of the world's newspapers and websites, he'd do it by making a big splash. And he knew exactly how he'd do it.

The only thing Fazil hadn't figured out yet was if he was willing to re-enter the fray, or if he'd wait and direct the operation in safe territory. He didn't consider the thought cowardly. To him, it was calculated, an approach he viewed as a pre-requisite to any serious planning.

Regardless of what he decided he would do, he was convinced of one thing: *The Americans are going to rue the day they came after me.*

CHAPTER 9

Paris, France

THREE DAYS HAD PASSED since Petrov duped Brady Hawk and the Firestorm team into doing her dirty work for her. She sat at her private table atop the balcony at Le 7th Ciel restaurant and sipped a glass of chardonnay. After all, such a victory deserved a moment of celebration, as short lived as it might be. There was still plenty of work to be done if she intended to see The Chamber's dream come to fruition. But baiting Hawk into murdering Germany's biggest bankers and then providing Interpol with footage of his assault was just cause to revel in her stroke of genius with some wine.

Anatoly slid Petrov's cigarette case toward her and held out his lighter.

She waved him off. "After dinner. I don't want to spoil my drink with my vice."

"Vice, as in singular?" Anatoly asked, the faint hint of a smile emerging across his face.

"Sophisticated women don't keep track of all their vices."

Anatoly held up his finger. "So it is plural. I was quite certain smoking wasn't the only vice you could claim."

"I could claim others, but they're far too unsavory to discuss in public," she said, leaning in close and dropping her voice to a whisper. "Seriously, who wants to talk about their penchant for murdering people who don't go along with all your suggestions. It makes you a bore at dinner parties."

"I can see how discussing your vices such as killing others could make you a bit of a pariah when you're out on the town with friends. The whole time they're wondering which one is going to be next."

Petrov patronizingly patted Anatoly's hand, which rested on the table. "There's a reason I hired a sharp-witted young man like yourself. You at least understand me."

"It's not that difficult."

"Pardon me."

Anatoly slunk in his chair, embarrassed that his comment slipped out. "That came out wrong. It's not what I meant. What I meant to say was—"

"Better quit while you're ahead, Anatoly. If you

keep digging, you might find yourself in a hole you can't crawl out of."

He nodded and sat up straight in his chair. "So, have you spoken with the leaders of the European Union Bankers Guild? They seemed really anxious to talk with you today."

"As a matter of fact, I was able to conduct a short discussion with several members. This whole fiasco in Germany has them running scared, as they should be. They're afraid of who might get hit next. Several countries have canceled their yearly gatherings."

"Private security getting too costly these days?"

Petrov shrugged. "And deadly. One agency I've contracted with in the past told me that they've lost six agents over the past twelve months."

"No wonder it's becoming such an expensive field."

"Yes, to risk your life for someone you don't know, there must be a handsome and commiserate financial award. Unfortunately, the recent events in Germany are creating a greater demand when the supply has reached its lowest."

"I trust your stunt in Stuttgart helped usher more players to the table," Anatoly said.

"They've practically come running, begging me to have a seat at the table," she said. "And of course,

I'm happy to oblige them as long as they abide by the set of rules laid out for them. Everyone needs to understand who is in control here."

"I'm confident that much is made clear."

Petrov reached out and snapped her fingers. Without hesitating, Anatoly handed her the cigarette case and held out a lighter. After she selected her smoke of choice, she leaned toward Anatoly, who flicked his lighter and waited for Petrov to get her vice sufficiently lit.

"I think it's also quite clear their precious financial institutions are all going to fail if they don't join The Chamber," Petrov said. "At this point, it's little more than a foregone conclusion, which is why they want to jump into the lifeboat I'm offering. The only thing they don't know is just how much it's going to cost."

"Not that they'll care."

Petrov forced a laugh. "Not that these types of people ever do. It's quite odd how money is no object to them, yet in the end, it's the only object they fancy. You'd think some of them might be happy to be relieved of such a burden, but that albatross hangs around their neck as if it's an adornment of fine jewelry."

"The Chamber will be more than happy to help ease such difficulties."

Petrov smiled. "Yes, we will."

She took a long drag on her cigarette before her phone buzzed. Picking it up, she waved it at Anatoly.

"If you'll excuse me, I need to answer this. My work is never done."

She slipped back inside and walked until she found a quiet hallway.

"I thought I gave you specific instructions not to ever call me at this number," Petrov said. Vadim, her top assassin, often ignored her directives, but she couldn't argue with his results.

"You also said to call you the moment I laid eyes on Hawk and his team," the man said. "It was quite the dilemma for me."

"You found them already?" Petrov asked.

"It didn't take long."

She laughed. "You're better than the FBI."

"That's not much of a compliment, if that's what you're trying to do there. They couldn't even gather enough evidence to—"

"It was meant to be a compliment, but I'm not going to explain myself."

"Better than the FSB would've been my preference."

"As a former KGB officer, I wasn't sure how you'd take that comparison."

"At this point, I don't care," Vadim said. "I simply

want to know how to proceed. Should I tip off the FBI so they can ride in like great American cowboys and take all the credit? Or would you like for me to handle it myself?"

"Where are they now?" Petrov asked.

"Getting questioned by airport security."

"So maybe the Americans won't bungle this thing in the end anyway."

"It would make their removal from play much neater."

Petrov sighed. "True, but I don't trust the American government either way. Follow them, and as soon as you get a chance, take them out in a remote location where you can get away cleanly. I don't want to let the narrative of these American rogue agents to get turned around on us. We're controlling this story so far—and it's turning into quite a beautiful one."

"No problem," Vadim said. "I'll take care of it."

"Good. Call me when it's finished."

CHAPTER 10

Washington, D.C.

HAWK STEADIED HIS BREATHING as his pulse quickened. His options were limited in such a public place. He could knock out the guard and hustle out of here, but that would leave an easily traceable trail. Hawk tried to keep his cool.

"Just heading home after a long flight," Hawk said.

The guard eyed him carefully, studying the access badge and Hawk's face equally.

"Everybody's gotta be a smart ass these days, don't they?" the man said.

Hawk took the question as rhetorical and refused to answer. It was clear by responding to the literal question the guard asked, Hawk put himself and the rest of his team at risk. Small talk wasn't Hawk's thing. He needed to get better at it for obvious reasons.

The guard held out the credentials and gently shoved them back. "Have a nice day," he said, waving Hawk through.

Hawk looked over his shoulder to see if Alex and Samuels were getting through hassle free. They were.

Once they were in the parking lot, Hawk flagged a shuttle down and rode it to the location he'd left his car. It wasn't registered under his name, but he thought it safe to take precautions and split up. Samuels and Alex waited for the next shuttle and rode it several minutes later. When they met back up, Hawk had the trunk open and was waiting for them to place their items inside.

"What did you do?" Hawk asked as he slammed his door shut. "Bat your eye lashes at him?"

Alex laughed softly. "I know you're jealous, Hawk. You might be able to gun a man down with a single shot from a thousand yards away, but you can't simply walk through a gated area without drawing a scrutinizing eye from a security guard. Admit it— you're jealous."

"What's there to admit? Those are both two great gifts to have in our line of work."

"Which is why you work together," Samuels said. "Now, can we put an end to the pettiness here and get on with it?"

* * *

HAWK DROVE WEST for about two hours until they arrived at a rural cabin nestled in the Shenandoah Mountains. After Blunt's last hideout was destroyed, he made it a priority to get another one that was more isolated with a single entry and exit point from the road. Blunt's assumption was that it would make an approach more difficult, though Hawk wasn't sure he agreed.

The cabin was about forty years old yet still in good condition. The wood slats on the outside had faded, but the structure was sturdy. Checking the perimeter, Hawk and Samuels circled their new temporary home.

"How long do you think we'll be here?" Samuels asked.

"Maybe a couple days or more," Hawk answered. "Depends on how quickly these threats begin to materialize."

"Think anyone will be able to track us out here?"

"I hope we'll be gone before they do."

Hawk collected a few thick branches and piled them to the side of the steps leading up to the house.

"I'm not sure starting a fire is a good idea," Samuels said.

"They're for whittling," Hawk said. "In case we get bored. Blunt isn't exactly the type to install an entertainment system here."

Samuels nodded and followed Hawk up the steps and into the house.

After they took the next half hour to settle in, they all convened at the kitchen table to discuss the information Hawk had sent them regarding the alliance between Petrov and Fazil. Hawk studied the information on the screen before he went slack-jawed.

"What is it?" Alex asked.

Hawk shook his head imperceptibly.

She prodded again. "Is there something we should be concerned about?"

"This information came from Commander Frank Stone at the Pentagon. Stone was my commander when I was with the Navy Seals. He's the one who gave the order to—"

Hawk's voice trailed off as he kept his eyes locked on the laptop.

"Are you okay?" Alex asked.

He blinked hard. "Just bad memories, that's all."

"So, how do you think Al Hasib is going about this attack?" Samuels asked, redirecting the conversation.

"Verge processes around 750,000 barrels of oil per day and is the country's main oil hub since the government assumed control of it," Hawk said. "And if I was a betting man, I'd put my money on Fazil orchestrating a fiery explosion. He wants visuals that will put Al Hasib back on the map."

They studied the schematics and discussed ideas for what that might look like practically.

"If I were wanting to make a splashy hit, I'd attack at several points," Hawk said. "Blowing the pipeline to pieces is one thing, but then you could get a black gusher spraying into the air if you hit the plant. And if they were really smart, they'd attack the controls that allow them to quickly shut off the flow remotely. Otherwise, they could set charges at several different points along the pipeline and turn this into another situation like when Iraq invaded to start the war in the 1990s."

"And you think the three of us will be enough to neutralize this attack?" Samuels asked.

"We're definitely going to need help on this one," Hawk said. "But the Kuwaitis are open to hearing from us. They're well aware that we care about them."

"Or their oil," Alex quipped.

"Doesn't make much difference," Hawk said. "That's all they care about, too."

"Well, I don't know about you two, but I'm famished," Alex said. "Why don't we get something to eat and then come back to finish planning how we'll stop them? Who's with me?"

"Let's go," Hawk said, jingling his keys.

"One of us needs to stay here," Samuels said. "Protocol."

Hawk nodded. "For once, I agree with you, Samuels. If our pictures have been plastered on television or social media, we shouldn't be out all together. We'll just pick something up and bring it back."

"I noticed a little deli on the edge of town a few miles back," Alex said.

"Perfect," Hawk said. "Let's go."

* * *

VADIM CROUCHED IN THE BUSHES, waiting for movement at the cabin. He'd tagged Hawk's car earlier, shooting a small tracking device at the bumper. It was how he'd been able to follow them to their location without getting made. It was also how he was going to kill his targets.

His legs had almost gone to sleep when he saw Hawk and Alex emerge from the cabin and head to their car. Vadim tugged the antennae out from the detonator and waited. While he was anxious to push the button, he hesitated once he realized a wrench had been tossed into his plan. Without all three of his targets in the vehicle, Vadim didn't want to invite a firefight in unfamiliar territory. He decided it'd be best to wait until they were down the road about a quarter of a mile before setting off the charge. That would enable him to verify the kills as he drove by and escape without drawing a tail from the third member of

Hawk's party. Vadim knew Petrov would be upset about not taking out all three, but Brady Hawk was the highest value target.

For a moment, he contemplated waiting for all three to get in the car but decided against it, unsure when or even if he'd get such an opportunity.

Vadim watched as a pair of car doors slammed and Hawk shifted the car into drive. Slipping through the woods, Vadim made his way down to the edge of the road, watching as their car disappeared over a hill. He then counted to himself.

Tree . . . dva . . . odéen . . .

He pushed the button, and his face lit up as he heard the car explode down the road.

* * *

HAWK HAD BARELY PUT HIS FOOT on the gas before his phone buzzed with a call from Samuels.

"You gotta get out of the car now," Samuels said.

"What are you talking about?" Hawk asked.

"I spotted what looks like an explosive device on the back as you were driving away."

"Who could've—?"

"Forget that. Just get the hell out of the car now before you're toast."

Hawk had just started to descend the hill when he slowed the car.

"Get out now and run," he said to Alex.

She didn't hesitate, following his lead. They both unstrapped their seatbelts and sprinted toward a ditch along the side of the road. Just as they reached a safe distance from the vehicle, it exploded.

Hawk put his head down and covered Alex's, protecting them from any falling shrapnel. After a few seconds, Hawk put his head up to inspect the damage. Instantly, the searing heat from the blast warmed his face to the point that he couldn't tolerate it more than a few seconds.

Hawk's phone buzzed again.

"Yeah," he answered.

"Thank God you're all right," Samuels said.

"I appreciate the heads up."

"Well, you're not out of the woods yet because I just saw a car roar out of here. Not that we can do anything about it since we don't have a viable mode of transportation."

"That's not entirely true," Hawk said. "If I'm not mistaken, Blunt told me he was keeping one of his old motorcycles up here."

"You better get moving if you don't want to lose him."

Hawk watched as a black Jeep roared past. Since the man refused to stop, Hawk assumed it had to be the assassin. Most people in this part of the woods would likely stop to see if they could help.

"Let's get back to the cabin," Hawk said to Alex. "I'm going to see if I can go after him."

Sprinting up the hill, Hawk made it to the cabin in less than a minute. It took him half that time to put on a helmet then rip the cover off the bike and kick-start it. Alex handed him a comlink as he prepared to leave. After pocketing the device, Hawk roared out of the storage shed and down the road in the direction he'd last seen the Jeep traveling.

Hawk shoved his hand between the side of his face and his helmet, jamming the comlink into place.

"Can you hear me?" Hawk asked.

"Loud and clear," Alex said.

"Okay, I need you to be my eyes on this one since I have no idea where he went."

"I'm hacking into the NSA database to get satellite imaging online right now, but I imagine he's going to be heading for the highest populated area in an effort to blend in and lose you."

"Well, let's make sure that doesn't happen, okay?"

"You're driving, chief," Samuels said.

Hawk grimaced. "Slap him for me will ya, Alex?" Hawk smiled as he heard a playful slap.

"What was that for?" Samuels asked.

"No pet nicknames for Hawk, got it?" Alex said.

Hawk approached a T-intersection. "Which way, Alex?"

"I can't see anything yet, but I'd go left. That's the fastest way back to the highway."

Hawk followed her instructions, accelerating quickly and speeding down the road.

"Watch out for the local deputies around here," Alex said. "I hear they can be quite the pain in the ass."

"The story of my life today," Hawk said. "But lately it's felt like that every day."

Silence for the next half minute as Hawk buzzed along the winding stretch of blacktop.

"Wait," Alex said finally. "I think I've got him . . . Yes, up ahead. He's turning left onto Pine Road."

"Got it," Hawk said.

Less than thirty seconds later, Hawk spotted the green Pine Road sign and turned hard left. He glanced at his watch, giving him an idea of how far behind he was from the Jeep.

I'm coming for you, bastard.

Hawk entered the edge of the small town that had been their original destination. The heart of the city was less than a mile from the highway, so Hawk knew if he could stay close to the assassin, he'd be able to catch him—especially since surprise was on Hawk's side.

Hawk maneuvered through the city at a slow pace, hoping no eager deputy spotted him and saw it as an opportunity to pad the community's coffers by issuing him a ticket for driving without valid plates. But that was the least of his worries. Getting a visual on the Jeep was his top priority, and he'd yet to accomplish that.

"Take a right onto Surrey Street," Alex instructed. "He's not that far ahead of you."

Hawk took the right Alex suggested and scanned the road ahead for the black Jeep. After a few seconds, he spotted the vehicle.

"I've got him," Hawk said.

"I'll keep monitoring everything on this end," Alex said.

Hawk was careful not to speed in an effort to both disguise his pursuit as well as not draw the attention of any local law enforcement. But it was killing him. He wanted to roar up to the assassin's window and deliver a quick kill shot and dig through his personal effects to find out who he was and working for. Yet, Hawk restrained himself.

Soon enough.

He went another quarter of a mile before he heard Alex screeching in his ear.

"What's wrong?" he asked.

"NSA just cut me out," she said. "You're on your own."

"No worries. I can handle it from here."

Hawk rolled up to a stop sign. Before he came

to a complete stop, he'd confirmed that the intersection was clear. But when he went to rev the accelerator, the engine sputtered.

"Come on, come on," Hawk said.

"What's wrong?" Alex asked.

Hawk glanced at the fuel gauge. It was pegged a half an inch below empty.

"Damn it, Blunt," Hawk said, pounding one of the handlebars. "I'm out of gas."

Hawk looked up and watched the Jeep turn onto the main road that led straight to the interstate.

CHAPTER 11

Washington, D.C.

PRESIDENT CONRAD MICHAELS hovered over the wet bar in his lawyer's office and pondered his choice of drink. After carrying on a rigorous debate in his head for several seconds, he finally settled on scotch over vodka. In the moment, his feelings toward the Russians were strong—and they weren't positive in any way.

"It's not even ten o'clock, Mr. President," Michaels's lawyer, Stan Fullbright said with a disapproving look. "You sure that's a good idea?"

"I have a few other ideas, but none of them are as good as this one," Michaels said, pausing to shrug. "Well, at least none of the other good ideas I have are legal."

"You could stand to keep the law on your side at this point," said Fullbright, who rubbed his protruding stomach. "Playing by the rules is your best option moving forward."

Michaels stared at his drink before taking a long pull. He sauntered around the room, stooping over periodically to inspect the pictures dotting Fullbright's wall. They were covered with government dignitaries from both the U.S. and abroad. The lawyer had become quite a political player over the years and was skilled at winning cases that the press deemed *slam dunks* in favor of the prosecution.

"You met Putin once?" Michaels asked, pointing at a photo depicting Fullbright and the Russian president together.

"I certainly didn't Photoshop him in," Fullbright said before he sighed. "Can we sit down and talk about your situation?"

"Did you like Putin? Did you find him trustworthy?"

Fullbright ignored him. "Do I need to remind you that I bill by the hour? And that I'm also the most expensive lawyer in Washington?"

"All right, you win," Michaels said as he took a seat across the table from Fullbright. ""What do you want to talk about?"

"I need to know how difficult my job is going to be here," Fullbright said. "You were a lawyer once. Is this case winnable?"

"Since it's not exactly a case, I absolutely think it's winnable. All we have to do is show the committee that there was no wrongdoing on my part."

"If there was, it won't be easy to bend the truth in your favor. The press is going to have a field day if we don't stick to a tight narrative that leads no room for interpretation."

Michaels drained the last of his scotch and set the glass down hard on the table. "I'll let you handle that as I prefer to keep my mouth shut."

Fullbright shook his head. "No, you're going to have to talk to the special investigator. If you don't, you'll look guilty."

"I don't want to perjure myself or give my political rivals ammunition in the next election."

"Be honest with me, Conrad," Fullbright said, studying Michaels carefully. "Is there a smoking gun I need to be worried about?"

"Of course not. This whole thing is a witch hunt. Some people just want to feel good about themselves—and they think ruining the political fortunes of a rival will do that. They're little people, and I have no patience for them."

"Whether you have patience or not, you need to demonstrate some as we move through this process. But you're going to have to put something on record."

"A public record?"

"I'll do my best to file a motion with the committee to make sure anything you say to the special investigator is suppressed publicly and sealed. Can you live with that?"

"I guess I'll have to."

Fullbright opened a folder and scanned several documents before continuing. "So, let's get to the biggest issue here—suppression of evidence. There's a recorded conversation between you and a Mr. Harry Bozeman where you discussed framing a U.S. operative if he didn't go along with your covert plan."

"We'll argue that the recorded conversation was taken out of context," Michaels said. "We were discussing issues of national security and methods of taking down a known terrorist who leads one of the most dangerous cells in the world, something we actually accomplished, by the way."

"I'm not sure everyone is going to see it that way."

"Context is everything. And it'll be a difficult case to make against me."

"Why is that?"

"Because I happen to know the only portion of that recorded conversation remaining is what was on that streamed Facebook video that slimy reporter ambushed me with."

"How do you—oh, never mind. It's probably best I don't know."

"Even with lawyer-client privilege?"

Fullbright took a deep breath and exhaled. "It's mostly so I can sleep at night."

Michaels rolled his eyes. "You're so noble, Stan."

"I don't have to take this case, Conrad. In fact, it's bad for business in the long run. Defending an unpopular sitting president for committing a crime against the republic? That's hardly my best career move."

"But we will win, and you'll be regarded as the hero—and there will be no end to the disgraced Washington bureaucrats beating down your door the moment they screw up. Perhaps you'll be able to increase your hourly rate after this."

"Fine, but you must come up with a reasonable explanation for that recorded conversation between you and Bozeman. And it's got to be one that can be public."

"I'll come up with something. Besides, it shouldn't take much. If President Clinton could beat a hearing by clarifying the definition of the word 'is,' I figure I should be all right."

Fullbright gathered the papers and stuffed them back into a folder. He then opened another one.

"Okay, on to the next order of business, the list of those the committee has requested to testify. It's a lengthy list, but I happen to know almost every one of them plans to refuse. Congress can't compel them, and they all have legitimate excuses. The ones who can't make it to the hearing but have agreed to meet with the special investigator all plan to plead the fifth on every question, so I think you're in the clear there."

"Excellent," Michaels said. "How did you? Oh, never mind. It's probably best that I don't know."

Fullbright cut a sideways glance at Michaels before continuing. "I think we're in the clear here as long as you're telling me everything."

"I am," Michaels said. "It was a poorly conceived plan; that much I'll admit. But there wasn't anything illegal about what we did. That operative survived as did the rest of his team. Besides, if the committee wants to make an issue out of that, I'll grill them for starting such a clandestine operation under my nose without my knowledge."

"But you knew—"

Michaels clucked his tongue and wagged his finger at Fullbright. "I knew nothing, remember?" Michaels smiled and stood. "I need to make some calls, but we'll continue this conversation tomorrow."

* * *

KATARINA PETROV'S EYES WIDENED as she glanced at the screen on her phone. She hadn't expected to hear from Conrad Michaels so soon.

"What a pleasant surprise," she said as she answered. "How are things coming along?"

"Better than expected."

"Is that so?"

"Yes, I appreciate your help in making those documents go away."

Petrov laughed softly. "Well, I'm afraid you're thanking the wrong person. I've barely had time to formulate my next move, let alone get one of my people to do your dirty work for you."

Michaels was silent for a moment.

"Conrad, are you still there?" she asked.

"Yeah, I'm here. Just wondering who might have done that and why."

"I'm sure you have plenty of friends in high places by this point in your career, do you not? It was likely someone there. But you can thank them for me, I suppose."

"Just another person to owe a favor to."

She smiled. "Just remember we're on the same side. You'll get what is owed to you in the end for your loyalty to The Chamber. Just be strong and weather the storm. If they don't have the tapes, they don't have anything."

"But what if we missed something?"

"You'll always miss *something*. Just don't let it be the main thing. As long as it isn't, you should be just fine."

"I'm counting on you to be true to your word."

"As am I," she said. "I'll be watching."

She hung up and snapped her fingers, arresting Anatoly's attention.

"Anatoly, I need your help."

"What is it?"

"Do you remember that document forger we worked with in the past?"

He nodded. "He wasn't the easiest person to work with."

"But his results were stellar, were they not?"

Anatoly shrugged. "No one ever figured out they were fake."

"He could be as obnoxious as a Hollywood starlet, as long as he produces a perfect document."

"I'm sure he can fulfill whatever request you have."

She held out her hand, waiting for Anatoly to offer her a cigarette. He obliged. Resting the butt gently on her lips, she eyed him closely and waited for him to offer her a light. She watched him fumble around in his pockets for one.

"Get him on the phone with me," she said. "I have a very important assignment for him."

CHAPTER 12

Shenandoah Mountains, Virginia

J.D. BLUNT WASTED little time in getting out to the cabin. He'd heard enough to make him nervous, even initially a little bit concerned. But when Alex explained Hawk had used Blunt's motorcycle to pursue the assassin, Blunt initially dropped his phone as he hobbled toward his car. He stooped down to pick the phone up and kept moving. Hawk wasn't being reckless, since Blunt's bike was the only vehicle available to maintain pursuit of the mystery man. However, it was still Blunt's bike, Blunt's baby.

He exited his car and hustled up the steps, tapping on the front door with his cane.

When the door swung open, Hawk, with a furrowed brow, was standing in the doorway.

"Back to using the cane again, I see," Hawk said.

Blunt grunted and pushed his way past.

"Take me to her."

"Alex?" Hawk asked.

"I want to see Matilda."

Hawk seemed confused. "I'm afraid there's no one on the Firestorm team by that name. Are you sure you're all right?"

"Matilda is the name of my bike. Take me to her," Blunt said flatly.

"This way," Hawk said, meandering through the house until they reached the back door. Walking down the steps and into the back yard, Blunt spied the storage shed, which was located about forty meters away from the house and held a wide variety of tools and supplies. Blunt's sole focus was to inspect his bike. He wasn't sure if he was going to beat Hawk with a cane or not, which happened to be the real reason Blunt had brought it along.

"Not a scratch on her," Hawk said as they arrived in the storage shed. "Just like the day you bought her."

Blunt stooped over and inspected Matilda more closely, running his fingers across the front chrome bumper. He climbed aboard and tested the seat.

"Apparently, it was much ado about nothing," Blunt finally said when he spoke.

"Your opinion or what other people suggested?" Hawk asked.

"Both."

"At least you're honest," Hawk said.

"Let's get back inside," Blunt said as he climbed off the bike. "We have a lot to talk about."

Inside the cabin, Blunt took a seat at the head of the table and waited for Hawk, Alex, and Samuels to join. To get situated, Blunt pulled out a cigar and started to chew on it.

"We're going to get you three out of here as soon as this conversation is done," Blunt announced. "I don't expect your little friend is coming back any time soon, but it won't matter because there's some pressing business that needs to be handled in the Middle East, namely Kuwait."

"We've been talking about that, Senator," Hawk said.

Blunt leaned back in his chair and folded his arms. "And what can you tell me?"

"If Al Hasib strikes Verge, it's going to be a mess in the desert," Samuels said.

"Oil prices are going to spike, and every member of OPEC is going to be up in arms and wanting to join us in the mission to hunt down Al Hasib," Alex added.

"So, good news, bad news?" Blunt asked.

"I think the fact that Karif Fazil is still alive can only be bad news," Hawk said. "We thought he was gone, but apparently that's just some good ole fiction."

A hint of a smile appeared on Blunt's face. "Well, I have to admire a man who can fake his own death."

"It's the staying dead part that's most important," Hawk said. "And I don't know if it was either his ego or Petrov's offer that brought him back from the grave, but either way it sounds like he's ready to return to wreaking havoc."

Blunt shrugged. "As best as I can tell, we still hold the upper hand."

"How do you figure?" Samuels asked.

"Fazil doesn't know that we know he's still alive," Blunt said as he uncrossed his arms and leaned forward. "He probably thinks his greatest weapon is surprise, but that will be muted when we meet him at his point of attack."

"Yeah, about that," Hawk said. "Hitting Verge is like throwing a rock in the ocean—you can't miss. There are so many vulnerable points along their vast pipeline, not to mention all the places they could target at the refinery. If Al Hasib manages to penetrate the perimeter, it could be raining oil for days over Kuwait City."

"It's not like the pipeline is unguarded," Blunt countered.

Alex nodded. "True, but Verge doesn't have enough personal contractors to withstand a siege like the kind Al Hasib is capable of bringing."

"The pipeline is a concern," Hawk explained. "Depending on where they attack and how damaged it is, Verge could have trouble shutting it down. However, it won't spill into the desert forever. At some point, it's going to run dry."

Blunt raised his eyebrows. "So, I take it you're more concerned about the refinery?"

Hawk nodded. "That seems to be the most vulnerable location and the place that would result in the greatest damage. Three quarters of a million barrels of oil per day would either be spilled or unable to be processed."

"But why now?" Alex asked. "Why does the attack seem so likely to happen in the next few days?"

"I know you probably haven't paid attention to the markets lately," Blunt began, "but they're tanking. After Petrov screwed us over and had you take out the leaders of Germany's financial sector, putting everything into a chaotic state, she sees this as her window of opportunity to gain control of the world markets."

"And how exactly is she going to do that?" Samuels asked.

"The same way she does everything else—bribes, blackmail, bullets, and bombs," Blunt answered. "There's little she can't accomplish without that combination. For whatever reason, she's chosen to escalate things now. Unfortunately, we have to act now."

"It'd be much easier if some Seals or other special ops unit went in on this program," Hawk said. "They could kick ass and be out of there before anyone knew what happened."

Blunt inspected the thick outer wrapping on the smoldering cigar for a moment. "I agree with you, but that's not going to happen in this political environment. The mood of the country is that we need to butt out of the Middle East, not to mention the fact that this is an overseas operation—and all of those have been temporarily suspended until this mess with Michaels gets sorted out."

"What about the Kuwaiti Guard?" Hawk asked. "Couldn't they at least provide some support?"

Blunt shrugged. "Perhaps, but they don't like to be shown up. They're also not very fond of having us rooting around in their backyard."

"They owe us," Hawk said.

"I think they've repaid that favor hundreds of times over," Blunt said. "But I'll make sure the message is passed along to them that we have evidence of a credible threat. I'll just fail to mention you're there."

"Gee, thanks," Samuels said. "Sounds like we're on our own."

Blunt nodded. "I can't exactly tell them we're sending you when you're supposed to be wanted by both the FBI and Interpol."

Hawk slapped Samuels on the back. "Welcome to the world of being expendable."

"This isn't what I signed up for," Samuels said.

"Take it up with Young," Blunt said. "For now, this is what you get. Now, I suggest you formulate a plan to stop the attack on the Verge refinery and figure out a way to survive."

Hawk shoved a clip into his gun and gave Samuels a wry grin. "Taking down terrorists is exactly what I signed up for."

"And it's time to get to it," Blunt said. "I'm getting a plane ready for you at Hyde Field. Everything you'll need for the mission will be there. Wheels up in four hours."

CHAPTER 13

Paris, France

KATARINA PETROV SLOWLY CIRCLED the table packed with financial leaders from countries all across Europe and the Middle East. With the way the banking system had been constructed, each leader had the power to make their currency rise or fall with the stroke of a pen. One investment here, one interest rate there—the moment the media took hold of the story capturing what move had been made, chaos ensued. The frenzied economic activity could be positive or negative. Petrov cared little which direction the indicators pointed in each country as long as everyone unwittingly ceded their power to Petrov.

"Gentlemen, what I want is a new currency, one that every country can fully support and trade," she said. "Look how well it went for Europe. The Euro maintains one of the strongest exchange rates on the open market, something that couldn't be said for many European countries before the move. Their currency was weakened, subject to the whims of the various decision makers. In some ways, the Euro has fool-proofed itself against the fluctuating market."

Hans Nilsson, the head of the Swiss Financial Market Supervisory Authority, lifted his hand. "You raise a good point, but certainly not the kind that will sway those in the European Union. If their currency is so strong on its own, why would they want to merge with you?"

"An interesting question from a man whose own country has refused to incorporate the Euro, a decision you no doubt regret," she said. "However, I understand what you're saying. And to such protests I say, 'Don't you want to be stronger?' It's nice to have a strong Euro, but it's still not the strongest currency in our global economy."

Ahmed Al Manahk, the head of the Kuwait Central Bank, stood. "And why exactly would we want to start another currency when ours is the strongest in the world?"

"Strong today, weak tomorrow," Petrov said. "What would happen if, say, all of your oil production was shut down or your oil fields began to dry up? Then what? Would the Kuwait Central Bank be able to boast such power in the market? I think not."

She lit another cigarette and continued talking. "The fact of the matter is we're strong together. All of us in this room can strike out on our own in hopes that we'll be able to avoid the inevitable disasters that befall every nation. And perhaps during your lifetime, you will. But what about those who come after you? Do you want future generations in your country to say your name with disgust or reverence? Will they see you as a visionary or a failed leader? Will you lift up future generations, or will you let them down? The choice is yours."

The room erupted in vigorous debate, men shouted back and forth across the table as to why it was nonsense, while others seemed eager to sign on for Petrov's plan.

"A one-world currency could reduce financial crime and create wealth for nations struggling to find it," one of the men said.

"Printing new money doesn't create wealth," another man countered. "Besides, Ms. Petrov isn't suggesting we give away this money as if it were candy in a parade, is she?"

Petrov held up her hand. "Absolutely not. There will be a minimum buy-in—and those who can't buy in immediately will be ushered in slowly until they have paid in the oldest currency on the market."

"You plan on using gold as the standard for this

currency?" another leader asked. "If so, count me in. Printing something on a piece of paper and acting as if it's worth something is what's ruining the market, country by country."

More vigorous debate ensued.

Petrov smiled faintly as she took in the scene. She blew a stream of smoke out of the side of her mouth as she watched the men bicker over the best way forward. As she paced, she noticed the door to the room swing open and, out of the corner of her eyes, saw Anatoly slip into the back. She walked over to him.

"What is it?" she asked in a low voice.

"I just received a call from two of our operatives wanting to know if you want them to proceed."

"Give them the green light and report back to me when the news picks it up," she said.

He nodded and scurried out of the room.

"So, gentleman," Petrov said, quieting the chaos for a moment while she walked back toward the table, "have you come to any consensus yet?"

The room sprang back into an uproar, making it clear to Petrov they were far from reaching a tentative unified decision. Any verbal decision today would need to be ratified by each country's governing bodies and wouldn't be something that could happen overnight. But Petrov was confident if she could gain momentum with such a large group of influencers, she'd see her dream realized soon.

For the next half hour, a robust discussion continued with the leaders debating the merits of each pathway. However, it all came to a crashing halt when Anatoly poked his head back in the door.

Petrov walked quickly over to him.

"Turn on the television," he said. "It will end all debate."

She hustled back over to the table and picked up a remote. She turned it on, flipping through the channels until she reached a popular cable news station.

On the screen, a forlorn anchor delivered the solemn report that more than a hundred were feared dead from a terrorist attack at the Madrid airport. On the screen beneath him, the ticker rolled past, providing updates of Spain's sudden collapsing financial markets. Then the anchor highlighted the loss of wealth from various stocks.

"Think you're all insulated from such an attack? Think again," Petrov said, delivering her final pitch. "So, who's ready to join?"

She smiled as more than ninety percent of the men in the room raised their hands.

This might be easier than I thought.

CHAPTER 14

Kuwait City, Kuwait

UPON ARRIVING IN KUWAIT, Hawk was greeted at the airfield by Chris Moore, a private security contractor who worked on a couple special projects for Blunt more than a decade ago. Moore handed the keys for a black armored Humvee to Hawk and helped load the team's equipment into the trunk.

"Seriously?" Hawk asked. "An armored Humvee?"

"Blunt was good to me," Moore said with a smile. "Still is."

Once they finished loading, Moore offered to drive and brief them along the way.

"How credible is this threat?" Moore asked Hawk after giving him an overview of the Verge oil refinery operation.

"We think it's real, but based off the last intel we

gathered, we can't be too sure," Alex chimed in from the back.

"We're here, so we're not taking it too lightly," Hawk said. "If this goes down, it's going to be a mess."

Moore nodded. "It took months to return oil production back to normal levels after the last attack."

"Do you know the head of Verge's security?" Hawk asked.

"He's a fellow employee, Doug Dorman. Works for Thunder House Security like me," Moore said. "But don't expect much out of him. He's an arrogant son of a bitch and views any government types like yourself as intrusive and unnecessary. He thinks everything runs more smoothly without Washington getting involved."

Hawk chuckled. "I second that notion, but we're not exactly sent here on orders from Washington."

Moore arched his eyebrows. "It was my understanding that Blunt authorized this operation."

"He did, but he's not exactly part of the Washington machine any more—at least, not officially anyway."

Moore threw his hands in the air. "Whatever, man. I don't care who's sending you here as long as you're affiliated with Blunt. It doesn't hurt that he's paying me to assist you."

"Good," Hawk said. "I'm going to need you to help us set up some visual surveillance around the facility and along the pipeline."

"That shouldn't be a problem."

"We also need to talk to this Dorman guy, make sure he understands we're not here to step on his toes."

Moore sighed. "This ought to be interesting."

* * *

THE TEAM TOOK TWO HOURS to rest and get situated in the house Moore rented for them for the week. Samuels stayed behind with Alex to get all the computer equipment fully functional. Moore rode with Hawk out to Verge's plant to get a quick face-to-face meeting with Dorman.

When they pulled up to the security office, Dorman was standing outside, hands on his hips, with a dark green hardhat on, chewing on a cigar. He barely acknowledged their arrival other than to swat at the dust cloud kicked up by the braking Humvee.

"Moore," Dorman said in a gravelly voice, "is this meeting really necessary? You know I'm going to say no to whatever it is you're asking for."

Hawk offered his hand. "Brady Hawk."

Dorman didn't move, glancing down at Hawk's hand. "Who is this newbie? He's way too enthusiastic to be from around here."

"He's the agent I told you about on the phone," Moore said. "They believe there's a credible threat to the Verge pipeline and facility that could occur within the next day or two."

Dorman laughed and crossed his arms. "What kind of credible threat are we talking about here? Certainly not one I've heard of."

"It came straight from the Pentagon," Hawk said.

"Oh, the Pentagon," Moore roared. "As if Washington doesn't have enough problems of their own that they have to come mucking around in our sandbox. Need I remind you that it was Washington that created this mess out here in the first place?"

Hawk took a step back. "Look, Washington didn't send me. It's complicated, but I'm not here to meddle in your operation. However, I am here to assure that Al Hasib doesn't turn Kuwait's sand black and take down the world's economy."

Dorman broke into a hearty laugh, taking his cigar out of his mouth. "You think something like that is going to happen on my watch? You're sorely mistaken. I've got some of the best trained security professionals in the world who could handle anything thrown at them."

"Normal sabotage, one-off attacks—sure," Hawk said. "I think you could defend against those, but that's not how Al Hasib operates."

"I didn't know Al Hasib even existed any more. I thought they went the way of the dinosaur."

"Well, they're back and itching to make a splash in Kuwait City by bombing the Verge facility."

Dorman shook his head. "That still makes no sense. From what I know, they used to get most of their funding through people making money off this pipeline. It'd be crazy for them to do that."

"Not if they're getting a new source of income. But I can't get into all that right now. All I can ask is that you trust me on this one."

Dorman put his hands back on his hips and rocked back and forth from his heels to his toes. "I'm afraid you traveled a long way for no good reason, Mr. Hawk. I'm not inclined to give carte blanche access to my facility to some wet-behind-the-ears operative, especially when you can't even tell me anything beyond your veiled statements."

Moore finally spoke. "Come on, Dorman. Hawk and his team are legit, certainly not fresh meat. They've taken out more than their fair share of terrorists."

Dorman scowled. "According to who? Them? Or is that just another piece of information they aren't at liberty to disclose?"

"According to a longtime friend of mine who supervises them."

"And who might that be?"

"J.D. Blunt."

Dorman's face relaxed, and he turned to look at Hawk, eyeing him closely. "You work for J.D. Blunt?"

Hawk nodded.

"Why didn't you say so in the first place? Blunt is a good friend of mine, too. He taught me the finer points of chewing on a cigar."

Hawk exhaled. "So, you're good with us assisting your security team over the next couple days to make sure we neutralize this threat?"

Dorman stroked his face with his hand and stared past Hawk. "I guess we can make that work. But I need to set up some clear boundaries. And you need to understand one very important thing."

"What's that?" Hawk asked.

"I'm in charge, no matter what. No engagement with hostiles unless I get the okay for it. Understand?"

"Absolutely," Hawk said.

"Good," Dorman said. "Let me connect you with one of my assistants who can get you everything you need."

After the meeting concluded, Hawk and Moore returned to the house to gather the rest of the team and set up additional motion detection cameras at key points along the pipeline near the oil production facility. Moore volunteered to drive farther out and set some up as far as two hundred kilometers away. Four hours later, Hawk was satisfied they had the surveillance equipment necessary to spot an attack, and they went back to the house to catch a few hours of sleep before monitoring the pipeline and facility during the night.

* * *

FIVE MINUTES PAST 1:00 A.M., the first motion detection alarm went off on Alex's machine.

"That didn't take long," Alex muttered while Hawk and Samuels scrambled out the door and into the Humvee.

The two men raced out to the point along the pipeline where the movement had been detected. Hawk peered through his infrared binoculars across the rising sands for a sign of the aggressors.

"I see them," Hawk said. "Three hostiles to the northwest."

Samuels looked in the direction Hawk suggested. "I see them too. I also see two hostiles in the northeast."

Hawk set down his binoculars and pulled out his sniper rifle.

"What are you doing?" Samuels asked. "Moore said we weren't to engage any hostiles without Dorman's permission."

"Have you ever heard the saying, 'Act now, ask for forgiveness later?'" Hawk asked.

"Yeah, but it's not exactly a wise rule of thumb to live by," Samuels said.

"It's appropriate now. Besides, I'll fire off a few warning shots while you call Dorman so you can let him know his pipeline is under siege."

Samuels called Dorman and filled him in on the situation, resulting in a flurry of expletives that Hawk could hear several feet away. After a few seconds of peace, Hawk broke the silence.

"You hung up yet?" Hawk asked.

"Dorman warned us not to shoot until his men arrived."

"Good for him," Hawk said before squeezing off several shots at the hostiles. He struck one in the head, while the other he hit in the chest.

"Did you get them both?" Samuels asked.

"Only one kill, from what I can tell."

Bright flashing lights bounced along the horizon near the refinery entrance, arresting Hawk's attention.

"Looks like the cavalry is on its way," he said.

"Hawk," Alex said over the coms, "there's more trouble north of you."

"How far north?"

"Maybe fifty kilometers or more. I'm having trouble getting an exact reading on your location."

"How many hostiles?"

"A dozen, maybe more. They're spread out, too.

Looks like about every five kilometers," Alex answered. "I'll update you if I see any new developments."

"What the hell?" Samuels asked. "It only takes one hole in the pipeline to create a leak."

"It takes days to fix each breach though," Hawk said. "Petrov wants to make sure this is a crater on the market graphs, not a blip."

"Dorman is gonna be pissed."

"And not just with them," Hawk said.

"What do you plan on doing?" Samuels asked.

"The refinery just became a sitting target," Hawk said. "Al Hasib is going to blow it to kingdom come if we don't get back and stop it."

Hawk and Samuels hustled back to the Humvee and roared past the caravan of Verge security vehicles tearing out across the desert.

"Get Dorman back on the line and find out who's guarding the refinery," Hawk said as their vehicle bumped along.

Samuels dialed Dorman's number and put the call on speaker.

"What is it now?" Dorman growled.

"Who's minding the refinery?" Hawk asked.

"I am."

"By yourself?"

"Well, yeah," Dorman said. "I can handle it."

"We'll be there in a minute. Keep your eyes peeled. The pipeline attack was just a diversion. The real prize is the refinery, and that's what they're coming for."

Hawk hung up, unwilling to give Dorman a chance to throw his meaningless weight around. Hawk cared only about the mission, which was thwarting Al Hasib's attack on Kuwait's prized refinery.

A few minutes later, Hawk roared up to the gate and buzzed it to gain entry. No response. Hawk hit the button several more times impatiently.

"Come on, come on."

Nothing.

"I ain't got time for this," Hawk said as he put his Humvee in reverse and backed up about thirty meters before stomping on the gas.

Hawk steered the vehicle straight toward the gate and ripped right through it. Lights flashed and sirens sounded, but not a single security guard came out to investigate.

"They're already here," Hawk said as he scanned the area.

With guns trained forward, Hawk and Samuels got out and surveyed the surroundings.

"Let's check the security station," Hawk said.

They crouched low as they sprinted across the grounds toward the office building where they'd previously met Dorman. Hawk opened the door slowly and peeked inside. Once he deemed the area clear, he motioned for Samuels to follow. Inside, they found Dorman slumped dead in his chair, two bullets to the chest, one to the head.

"We've got to hurry," Hawk said.

They rushed back outside and scanned the facility for any movement.

"Up there," Hawk said, pointing toward one of the distillation towers.

Samuels squeezed off a couple shots before fire was returned. The two operatives hustled behind one of the parked security vehicles to regroup.

"I saw another hostile opposite the one you spotted," Samuels said.

"So, there are at least two of them."

"I'm guessing more than that."

Hawk peered around the corner of the front fender, only to be greeted by two more shots that peppered the ground.

"I'm going up after the one on the left," Hawk said. "You take the guy on the right."

"But we don't have any cover," Samuels argued. "We're going to be sitting ducks."

"And this place is going to be awash in oil if we don't make an attempt to take action."

Hawk didn't wait for a reply. He stole across the

grounds, ducking behind vehicles and holding tanks as he moved toward the tower. He stealthily climbed the ladder, stopping at a platform to see if the Al Hasib operative above had taken notice. If he had seen Hawk, the man wasn't acting like it.

Hawk glanced across at the other tower, where Samuels started to climb. Above Samuels, the hostile was busy staring at the explosive device in his hand and had his back turned to Hawk. Seizing the opportunity, Hawk fired off a shot, hitting the man in the back. He plummeted to the ground.

The man above Hawk moved frantically over him, shooting down at Hawk. Samuels fired two shots and took the man out. Hawk watched as the man toppled over the railing and hit the ground with a thud.

"Nice shot, Samuels," Hawk said over the coms.

"I don't think we're out of the woods yet," Samuels said. "Look over there on the holding tanks. There's at least a dozen flashing devices from what I can see."

"Alex, are you seeing all this through the security camera feeds?" Hawk asked.

"It's hard to see since these cameras don't have much definition," she said.

Hawk raced back down the steps and studied the explosive device lying next to one of the dead Al

Hasib agents. "These devices look like they're radio controlled—and there's way too many of them around the facility for us to take down at this point."

"Can you open one up for me?" she asked.

"I'll see what I can do."

Hawk and Samuels rushed back to the security building and found a toolbox in the maintenance closet. Hawk dismantled the casing and turned on his body camera to show Alex the device.

"Perfect," she said after a few minutes. "I can jam the signal, piggybacking off a cell tower located less than a kilometer from where you are."

"I don't need an explanation," Hawk said. "Just do it quickly. We have no idea how much time we have left." He turned toward Samuels. "We've still got some work to do out here. Follow me."

The two men went to the front of the security building and crept out into the open. As they dashed toward cover, a loud flash and explosion went off near their feet.

Hawk flew up in the air and then landed hard on his back.

He was still unconscious when the pair of Al Hasib operatives dragged him toward their truck and threw him next to Samuels.

CHAPTER 15

Washington, D.C.

PRESIDENT CONRAD MICHAELS tried to remain composed as he stood at the podium. Staring out across the Washington press corps, he struggled to see as flash bulbs popped and what seemed like a thousand reporters all tried to ask him questions at once. His wife squeezed his hand. He forced a faint smile as he glanced at her putting on a brave face. It wasn't the first time she'd been there for him. He certainly hoped it wasn't the last.

He released her hand and took hold of the podium, just as his speech coach had directed. The coach suggested Michaels needed to exude strength and demonstrate to the American people he was still a powerful leader. It was a familiar position Michaels found himself in again after the latest leak that hit the press, this time the accusation he and his wife had committed tax fraud.

Michaels held up his hands to silence the anxious reporters all frothing at the mouth to get their questions answered. He waited until the room was quiet with the exception of clicking cameras.

"When the news broke yesterday that Bethany and I had committed tax fraud, I considered not even responding," he began. "The unfounded allegations are so outrageous that I told my council I didn't want to legitimize them by even talking about them. But over the past twenty-four hours, it was clear this wasn't just a passing item in the news cycle. So, I was encouraged to address the issue directly before anything more could be made of it."

Michaels swallowed hard and adjusted the papers in front of him before returning his hands to the side of the podium.

"The documents that have been widely circulated in the media, likely against the advice of any good lawyer, are fakes. They will be proven to be fraudulent as an independent digital forensics expert has already demonstrated. But that hasn't stopped the detractors from attempting to take down my presidency. I have full confidence this latest pack of lies will be put to rest in the next few days along with the senate committee's investigation into any wrongdoing in our attempts to catch one of the world's most renowned terrorists. I look forward to getting back to serving the

American people and helping us move forward as a nation united around the values that make this place the greatest country in the world. Thank you for your time today."

Michaels stepped back from the podium as the throng of reporters shouted questions. He waved and flashed a few thumbs up signs before striding off the stage while holding his wife's hand.

"A bunch of savages," Michaels muttered once they stepped behind the curtains.

Michaels's speech coach closed his eyes and sighed, shaking his head slowly. Despite being reminded constantly, Michaels had forgotten that his microphone was still hot.

"Congratulations," the coach said. "You just created another controversy with that statement."

Slack-jawed, Michaels stared at his wife.

"It's your bed, honey," she said. "You made it; you lie in it."

Michaels cracked his knuckles then clenched his fists. "I need a drink."

CHAPTER 16

Paris, France

KATARINA PETROV STOOD at the doorway to her penthouse suite and welcomed the president of the European Central Bank, Henri Dubois. She offered him a drink, which he readily accepted. After making him a martini, she sauntered across the room to speak with Anatoly.

"I'll take it from here," she said.

"Are you sure? I can stay near the bar in case you need me for anything else," he said.

"No, I'll be fine. You just go find out why nothing has happened in Kuwait yet. Let Fazil know I'll withhold payment until the job has been completed."

Anatoly rocked from side to side, shifting his weight from one foot to the other. "I'm not sure I'm comfortable doing that. Fazil can be a—"

"Do it," she growled. "No more excuses. Do you understand?"

He nodded and retreated to another suite he'd reserved.

She spun back toward Dubois. "Now, where were we?"

Dubois flashed a smile. She knew he was used to getting what he wanted and expected nothing less out of their meeting. Petrov mulled how she would break the news to him: Dubois not only wasn't getting what he wanted, but he was going to give up much more than he ever anticipated.

"I think we were at the part where you were about to invite me to lead this dream you have of transitioning the world over to a new currency," he said, raising his eyebrows before taking a long sip of his drink.

She wagged her finger at him. "Walk with me." Petrov meandered out onto the terrace and promptly pulled out a cigarette.

"Smoke?" she said, offering Dubois one.

He waved her off. "I stopped years ago."

"Why?" she asked as the tobacco crackled and came to life. "If I didn't have these, I don't know how I'd manage all the stress in my life. I can only imagine your stress level is a thousand times greater than mine."

"I prefer alcohol as a way to calm my nerves," he said, raising his glass.

She laughed softly. "I don't like to discriminate. Whatever vice works, I'm all for it."

"I hope your lack of discrimination ends at your vices," he said.

"Please explain yourself."

"I just meant that I hope you don't intend on tossing the European Central Bank members in with the rest of the dregs of your currency experiment," he said, his chin rising high as he spoke. "We've gone to great lengths to ensure the ECB is immune to any major worldwide recessions—well, as much as it can be."

Petrov turned and looked out across the city. "I actually wanted to meet with you to discuss what you could do for me."

"What I could do for you? You mean aside from getting the entire ECB to ditch the Euro and put our members in a more tenuous position by going with your plan to create a world currency?"

Petrov remained calm. "You sound as if you're considering changing your mind, Henri."

He furrowed his brow and stared at her. "You sound as if you're trying to push me into a corner. And do you know what a bull does when it's pushed into a corner?"

"You're no bull," she said before she sent a plume of smoke into the air.

"If you think you can have your way with me because of my past, think again," he said. "That's old news. Everyone has accepted my mistakes and moved on."

She continued to look straight ahead, refusing to look at him. "You're right, Henri. It is old news. I'm not interested in dredging up your sordid past. But I am interested in getting you to meet some of my demands on this issue. No, let me rephrase that: I am confident you'll see things my way. Besides, if you don't, your successor has already expressed that he's much more open to my ideas than you are."

Henri narrowed his eyes. "What are you suggesting?"

She reached into the pocket of her blazer and then handed him a stack of three photos, all obviously taken secretively. Slowly, she turned to see his expression.

Mouth agape, Dubois studied the photos one by one. "I can't . . . How could you . . . ? What is the meaning of all this?"

"Henri, you're the one who lectures everyone about the importance of *family*," she said as she moved directly in front of him. "Perhaps your wife would like to see just how broadly you define that word."

"This is outrageous," Dubois said as he eyed Petrov, turning his back to the view of the cityscape. "If you think this is how you're going to get me to acquiesce to your ridiculous requests, think again. No, in fact, forget it. I'm pulling the ECB out of this deal. We're not going to join you."

"Is that so?"

"Yes," he grumbled as he ripped up the photos.

"You might want to reconsider your position."

"The position of the ECB has officially changed, and it's not changing back," he said as he glared at her.

With a sharp move toward Dubois, Petrov managed to catch him off balance as he tried to move out of the way. She gave him a forceful shove, one he wasn't expecting.

When the back of his knees hit the railing, they buckled and he folded—only the weight of Dubois's momentum had already sealed his fate. He fell backward and tumbled over the edge.

Petrov peered down to catch a glimpse of him flailing and screaming, eyes wide with fear. The last thing she heard him say was, "How could you?" Then a terrible thud against the cobblestone street below.

"He shouldn't have been too quick to resist me," Petrov said as she walked across the veranda and back into her suite.

CHAPTER 17

Somewhere in the Persian Gulf

WHEN HAWK REGAINED consciousness, he kept his eyes closed. It was the only chance he had to get a feel for his surroundings before the guards chatting above noticed he was awake. Hawk expected dismal treatment from the Al Hasib terrorists if he even managed to survive the night.

Hawk breathed in through his nose. The saltwater aroma was stronger than it had been in Kuwait City. That combined with the swaying motion led him to believe he was on a seafaring vessel. With his hands lying limp beside him, Hawk rubbed the floor, which was made of steel. It certainly confused his senses. If he hadn't smelled salt water, Hawk would've sworn he was lying in the back of a truck. But he couldn't ignore that or the sound of circling seagulls just outside.

Cracking his eyes open ever so slightly, he imagined to see a skyline. Instead, all he saw was a sky with a faint smattering of stars nearly muted by the glow of city lights in the distance. Then he heard the splashing of water.

Definitely in a truck on a boat.

It was a new experience for Hawk, but he wasn't surprised. The quickest way out of Kuwait City was by boat. If he were to spring a surprise attack, he'd likely have followed a similar route.

Hawk scanned the truck and noticed the guards weren't paying him any attention. The two who'd been assigned to watch the captured Americans were staring at cell phones.

Hawk turned slightly toward Samuels and nudged him. Samuels moved cautiously and barely opened his eyes. Hawk used his eyes to gesture toward the guard above Samuels.

"On three," Hawk mouthed. "One, two, three."

With their wrists still tied together, Hawk and Samuels sprang to their feet and used their bound hands like battering rams, delivering several wicked punches to the faces of the shocked guards. They never even had a chance to fight back. Once the men were knocked unconscious, Hawk and Samuels helped each other out of their bindings before they exchanged clothes with the guards and returned them to the prisoner position.

"Where are we?" Samuels whispered.

Hawk glanced at one of the men's watches. "We haven't been out that long. I'm going to guess somewhere off the coast of Kuwait in the Persian Gulf."

"And where do you think they're taking us?"

"Hopefully back to their compound," Hawk said with a smile.

Samuels shook his head. "You're one sick man, Brady Hawk. I mean, I'm all for getting dropped into the hornet's nest so we can eradicate these bastards, but do you think we'll be able to survive something like that? I doubt it. I say we run now."

"More like swim. We've literally got nowhere to run, so we might as well enjoy the ride and see what happens."

"You have a nose for danger. Do you know that?"

"Know that? I pride myself in that," Hawk shot back. "It's the only way I know how to live. It's what keeps me alive."

"There's something wrong with that statement, but I'm not going to argue with the results. We're still alive, if only for a few more hours."

Hawk playfully punched his partner in the arm. "Don't look so depressed, Samuels. It's not fun unless there's some risk involved. And this might be the riskiest thing I've ever done."

"Didn't Alex mention you escaped capture from Al Hasib in the past?"

"Perhaps," Hawk said. "It's become routine."

"Then why haven't they killed you yet?"

"Good question. Let's ask Karif Fazil that in person when we find him."

Samuels exhaled and shook his head. "You're certifiable."

"I've been called worse."

Five minutes later, the vessel slowed down. By this point, Hawk had been able to ascertain they were on a private ferry. He'd managed to poke his head out of the back and identify several military-style vehicles.

"This is Al Hasib, all right," Hawk said to Samuels. "They're going to take us straight to Fazil."

"Got any idea where we are yet?"

Hawk strained to read the sign near the dock. "I'm guessing we're on Failaka Island."

"Failaka Island?"

"Yeah, about a thirty-minute ferry ride off the coast of Kuwait City."

"This is where Al Hasib set up operations for this attack?" Samuels asked. "Doesn't seem like the most efficient location to me."

"No, but it's definitely where you'd want to go if

you didn't want to get caught. They can zip out of here in a hurry while the rest of the poor sots on the mainland would be left as martyrs for the cause."

"Why don't we end their cause?"

Hawk smiled. "I'm all for that. Just follow my lead."

When the boat finally docked, the vehicles filed out onto the mainland, forming a small convoy. Hawk observed six trucks rumbling along with their vehicle being at the end.

"I can't believe they wouldn't put the prisoner transport in the middle," Hawk said.

"It's definitely not by the book," Samuels said.

"Maybe Al Hasib doesn't have a book."

"My head would explode."

Hawk flashed a grin. "Well, just so you know, everything we're about to do is against the book. Instead of being quiet and maintaining our story in an interrogation setting, we're never going there."

"Roger that."

After a few more minutes, the convoy started to slow until they came to a halt in a makeshift camp along a deserted beach on the western portion of the island. Two boats were anchored just offshore while a pair of wooden transport rafts were anchored on the beach.

A flurry of activity brought the dimly lit camp to

life as the men began running around and unloading equipment. It was so chaotic that no one noticed Hawk and Samuels drag the two men who'd been in the cab of their truck into the back and knock them out. Hawk and Samuels kept their heads down and toted munitions boxes to a staging area along with the rest of the men. Then Hawk saw something that caught his eye.

"Do you see what I see?" Hawk asked.

"I see him," Samuels said. "If I wasn't following your lead, I would've already put a bullet in Karif Fazil's head."

"Wait. You see Fazil?"

Samuels scanned the area. "Well, I did see him. He's gone now."

"I was talking about Lee Hendridge, the American journalist who'd been captured about a week ago. We've got to take him with us."

"Screw that," Samuels said. "Our mission is all about Fazil. We need to take that bastard down, no matter what."

"I don't want to argue about this now, but we won't be able to kill Fazil and get out of here alive. But we can get Hendridge safely out if we operate cautiously."

"You're crazier than you look, Hawk. I'm not sure I like this plan."

"If you don't go along with me on this, you're on your own."

"Fine, but I'm laying the blame all at your feet when we meet with Blunt."

Hawk laughed. "When we meet with Blunt—I like your attitude. Keep it positive, okay?"

They made a couple more trips between the truck and the staging area, carting the munitions boxes, until Hawk saw the opportunity to free Hendridge and attempt an escape.

"You sure about this?" Samuels asked.

"I'm never sure about anything until I try it."

Hendridge was bound and gagged, standing against a pole next to one of the hastily erected tents. A guard standing near Hendridge had left, leaving the journalist free for the taking.

Hawk ripped through the ropes quickly, while Samuels removed the gag from Hendridge's mouth.

"Who are you guys?" Hendridge whispered. "I hope you're know what you're doing or you're going to get us all killed."

"Just stay calm, kid," Hawk said. "We're gonna get you out of here. Just stay low and follow me."

The trio crouched low and moved swiftly across the camp, staying in the shadows. Hawk directed them toward a truck, instructing them to get in the back. He slid into the front seat behind the wheel and checked for the keys. They weren't here. He checked the visor. Nothing.

Hawk noticed a small knife sitting on top of the console. He snatched it and used it to strip several wires beneath the steering wheel in an attempt to hotwire the truck.

He froze when he heard the jangling of keys and a clipped sentence in English.

"Looking for this?" the man asked.

Hawk looked up and was met with a vicious blow to his face.

CHAPTER 18

Washington, D.C.

J.D. BLUNT WAS ENJOYING a cup of coffee and reading the latest commentary on Michaels's botched press conference when his phone buzzed. Glancing at the screen, Blunt sighed and put down his newspaper.

"I hope you have a good report for me," Blunt said as he answered.

"Well, you didn't hear about the Verge refinery plant exploding across the sands of Kuwait, did you?" Alex said.

"No, I didn't," he said. "However, I saw something about a thwarted attack. I'm guessing you're calling with good news."

"Good and bad."

"Good news first?"

"I already gave it to you," Alex said.

"Where's Hawk?"

"That's the bad news. He and Samuels are gone."

"What do you mean *gone*?"

"I mean *poof*, thin air, gone. Nobody can find them, and it hasn't been easy to get any answers out of Verge since Doug Dorman was killed in the attack."

"Damn it," Blunt said. "Doug Dorman was a good man."

"You knew him?"

"We worked together a few times. He was a hard ass sometimes, well, more like all the time, but he was one of the good guys."

"He's also one of the latest casualties from Al Hasib's attempted strike. And from what I can gather, they might be preparing to make another attack."

"You sure about that?"

"I guess we'll find out, though I heard Verge has beefed up its security considerably since then."

"They'd be fools not to," Blunt said.

"But Verge still hasn't cleared all the explosives. I've been jamming the radio frequencies here since the attack to make sure Al Hasib can't detonate anything and make this worse than it already is."

"Keep it up. I'll make some calls, see if I can get some help. Do you have Hawk and Samuels's last location?"

"Some pier in the harbor, so they could be anywhere by now."

"All right, I'll be in touch."

Blunt hung up and called Frank Stone.

"Frank, I need your help with something," Blunt began. "I've lost two agents, and I need you to get them."

"The two agents wanted by Interpol and the FBI? You've got some nerve, J.D.," Stone said. "I mean really."

"Look, this isn't the time to get into a pissing contest. We've got two of our top operatives in danger right now, and I need an assist."

Stone laughed. "If they're your top operatives but got captured by a bunch of local bandits from Al Hasib, I'd say you're throwing around labels far too generously. Maybe you need to reassess how you define the word *top*. I'm not touching this one," Stone said.

"Why the change of heart, Frank?" Blunt asked. "You're the one who asked me for help on this in the first place."

"Yeah, but I was expecting you to get someone to do the job and do it right, not screw it all up and have it come back on me."

Blunt was seething on the inside but tried to remain calm as he responded. "You know how it is on the battlefield. Sometimes you get into a situation that you didn't expect or never could've accounted for."

"Yeah, and when that happens, you die. End of story."

"These men are worth going after."

"Maybe for you, but I'm not willing to risk my career over them."

"What's gotten into you, Frank?"

"The bottom line is I know who hired you, and Noah Young isn't going to be President much longer. And while Michaels won't hear it from me, some other eager beaver ready to ascend to the ranks of power will spill the beans, and you'll be screwed. That much I can promise you. It won't be pleasant by any stretch of the imagination."

"So, I guess that's a no on helping Brady Hawk."

"It's a *hell no*, J.D. And you only have yourself to blame. You should've selected a more competent agent."

Blunt hung up his phone and started to pace around the room. He needed some help—and fast.

CHAPTER 19

Kuwait City, Kuwait

HAWK FELT SAND POURING into his boots, his arms dragging along the ground as an Al Hasib operative pulled him into a tent. With orders being barked out, Hawk barely opened his eyes in an attempt to survey the situation more properly. Another guard lugged Samuels toward the tent in the same manner. But that was the extent of the Al Hasib muscle assigned to watch the pair who'd attempted an escape and failed.

Guess we deserve that.

Samuels began moving around before he mumbled something, drawing the ire of the guard towering over him. Screaming and cursing, the guard dropped Samuels for a moment, kicked him in the ribs, and then picked him back up.

At least I know he's awake now.

Convinced escape would only become increasingly more difficult the longer they were held hostage, Hawk sprang into action. He grabbed the guard's arms and pulled downward. The guard, who was already hunched over Hawk, lost his balance and toppled headfirst to the ground. Still holding onto the guard, Hawk used the man's momentum to spring upward. The guard who'd been pulling Samuels spun around, surprised at the sudden tussle. He barely got a word out of his mouth in a call for help before Hawk delivered a vicious kick to the man's knees, sending him sprawling toward the ground. Samuels clamored to his feet and attacked the guard while Hawk returned his attention to the other operative. Another roundhouse kick and a pair of targeted punches knocked the guard unconscious. Hawk knelt beside the guard to search for his keys. Meanwhile, Samuels took care of the other guard.

"Ready to make another run for it?" Hawk asked.

"Only if you've got the keys this time, Einstein," Samuels quipped.

Hawk held them up triumphantly and jangled them before snatching the man's gun from his pocket. "I rarely make the same mistake twice."

"Just be glad that mistake didn't cost us our lives."

"Let's get outta here," Hawk said as he crept near the entry to the tent.

"Where's Hendridge?" Samuels asked.

"Let's see if we can find him on the way out," Hawk said.

The camp was still in a state of chaos as men scurried back and forth, carrying equipment and loading it onto trucks, as if they were breaking camp.

Still disguised by their insurgent fatigues, Hawk and Samuels kept their heads down as they weaved through the other soldiers too focused on their task to notice the escapees.

"Over there," Hawk whispered. "I see Hendridge."

"What's he doing?"

"Looks like they've got him tied up to something."

"I'll cut him free, and we'll get the hell out of here for real this time."

"But—"

"Save it," Hawk growled. "You take the keys to the truck, and I'll meet you there."

Samuels reluctantly took the keys from Hawk's hand as they broke ranks. Keeping his head down, Hawk walked swiftly over to Hendridge and cut him free in one smooth motion.

"Keep your hands behind your back like you're still tied up," Hawk said, yanking Hendridge to his feet. "We're going to make it out of here this time."

Hendridge followed Hawk's instructions and marched across the grounds another thirty meters until they reached the row of transport trucks. Hawk found Samuels sitting in the driver's seat of one.

"Ready to go?" Hawk asked.

Samuels nodded and attempted to insert the key into the ignition, but it didn't fit.

"Damn it," Samuels said. "This is the wrong truck."

Hawk opened the driver's side door and slapped at the visor up above. The keys slid down and into Samuels's lap.

"How did you—?"

"Lucky guess. It's what I should've done last time."

Samuels turned the ignition, and the truck sputtered before it roared to life.

"Now let's the hell outta here," Hawk said as he shoved Hendridge toward the back of the truck. They had barely finished piling in before Samuels jerked the truck into gear and started rolling.

Despite the activity around camp, several soldiers noticed the truck moving and began yelling. Then shots were fired.

Hawk ducked as he pushed Hendridge's head down in an effort to keep them both safe below the tailgate. Shots pinged off the truck, and more men yelled as the truck increased speed. After a few more seconds, Hawk decided to look up and see what was happening. When he did, the scene wasn't one he expected.

Three men were less than a meter away from the back truck and were preparing to grab hold of the gate and climb aboard. Hawk wasn't having any of it. He shot two men before the third guy managed to get onto the truck's bumper and kick the gun from Hawk's hand. The man climbed aboard and whipped out a knife.

The truck continued rambling forward, bouncing up and down as Samuels struggled to avoid the pothole-laden stretch of road. Both Hawk and the attacker fought to maintain their balance, while Hendridge slunk into the corner near Hawk.

"Just stay there," Hawk said to Hendridge, pointing at the corner while focusing on the man.

The man lunged at Hawk, who managed to sidestep the charge. Hawk pushed the man backward, sending him stumbling toward the side of the truck. Once he regained his footing, the man charged Hawk again. However, Hawk slid to the side, only this time, he seized the man's arm, forced it down in an effort to shake the knife loose. When that didn't work, Hawk spun around behind the man and wrestled him, forcing the blade to point at the attacker. The Al Hasib operative resisted for nearly half a minute before Hawk succeeded and drove the knife into the man's midsection.

He screamed and relinquished the knife in an instinctive attempt to stop the bleeding. That was all Hawk needed to finish the man off and give him a quick death. Snatching the knife off the floor, Hawk slit the man's throat and hurled him out of the back of the truck.

"Are you okay?" Hawk asked Hendridge.

Hendridge nodded. "I thought that was the end."

A faint smile appeared on Hawk's face. "We both got lucky today."

A distant buzzing sound froze Hawk in place.

"What is that?" Hendridge asked.

Hawk held up his hand and craned his neck to hear. It was a distinct sound he knew all too well.

"Drone strike," Hawk said.

"Drones?" Hendridge said. "What if we were still there?"

"Casualties of war—but thank God we're not."

Twenty minutes later when they reached the docks, Hawk convinced a man to take them back to the mainland with the promise of a handsome payday. At first the man wasn't interested, but Hawk doubled his offer once they reached land, convincing the captain to change his mind.

Once they were back in Kuwait City, Hawk and Samuels took Hendridge to their safehouse to meet up with Alex.

"Thank God you're okay," Alex said. "After I lost contact with you, I wasn't sure what happened."

"Did you give Blunt our position?" Hawk asked.

She nodded. "He told me he had someone who could help us out, maybe get an extraction team in there."

"Well, I have a bone to pick with him then because someone sent a drone strike to the camp."

She slammed her fist on the table and let out a string of expletives. "Every time I think Blunt is on our side, he pulls some stunt like this."

"Agreed," Hawk said. "Let's get the bastard on the phone right now."

Alex dialed Blunt's number and handed the phone to Hawk.

Hawk dispensed with any pleasantries when Blunt answered and put the call on speaker. "What was the meaning of sending in a drone strike to our location?"

"Drone strike? What the hell are you talking about?" Blunt asked incredulously.

"Samuels and I were stuck in an Al Hasib camp when a drone strike was called in. Fortunately, we were on the way out of there when we heard the buzzing."

"*Sonofabitch*," Blunt muttered. "That Frank Stone."

"Did you tell Commander Stone where we were?" Hawk asked, his voice rising.

"I gave him your coordinates because he said he could get an extraction team in there to pull you out. I had no idea he'd—"

"Be careful around that guy," Hawk said. "I don't trust him."

"I don't trust him fully, but I didn't think he'd pull something like this," Blunt said. "But never mind that for now. Catch me up to speed on the status at Verge."

"I think the threat has been averted for now," Alex said. "Al Hasib managed to inflict some damage, but from the reports I was able to gather, it won't keep the oil production down for more than a couple days. From the report I heard, they already have repair teams out on the line."

"Good because you need to get some rest," Blunt said. "I've got another pressing assignment for you."

"Unless it involves Katarina Petrov—" Hawk began.

"It does," Blunt snapped. "We have some credible intel that she's flying a number of The Chamber board members to a private retreat out of Paris in a couple days."

"And what do you want us to do about it?"

"I want you to shoot the plane down, pin it on Al Hasib," Blunt said. "I've got all the details worked out."

"And we're the only ones who can do this?" Samuels asked.

"Blowing up a plane on takeoff is hardly an operation we want to have run by agents who can be traced back to the U.S.," Blunt said. "You three, on the other hand, are—"

"Expendable?" Hawk said, finishing Blunt's comment.

Blunt sighed. "I was going to say our best trained covert force located overseas."

"Toe-may-toe, tah-mah-toe," Hawk said. "We know how this works by now."

"As long as you're on board and get the job done, I don't care what you think," Blunt said. "I just want Katarina Petrov dealt with once and for all."

Hawk glanced at Alex. "You okay with that?" he whispered.

She nodded. "It's for the best."

Hawk looked back at the phone. "We do have some good news for you, too."

"I could use some."

"We rescued Lee Hendridge, *The New York Times's* journalist Al Hasib recently snatched. He's here with us."

"How did you manage that?"

"Long story," Samuels said. "It involved a bit of luck."

"I'll take it—and I'll send a plane to bring him home first thing in the morning. Sound good?"

Hendridge broke into a wide grin. "Sounds fantastic."

Hawk ended the call and stared sternly at Hendridge. "Not a word about this to anyone. You should've never been let in on that conversation, but I'll deny any of it being true if you ever report about it."

"I'm just happy to be alive," Hendridge said.

"Good. As long as we're all on the same page about this," Hawk said. "Now, let's get some rest. Sounds like Blunt intends to work us until we drop while we're fugitives."

CHAPTER 20

Washington, D.C.

CONRAD MICHAELS TOOK ANOTHER SIP of his water and shifted in his seat. He straightened his tie and leaned forward in his seat. Tugging the microphone closer, Michaels cleared his throat before he spoke.

"I'm sorry, sir," Michaels said. "Can you please repeat the question?"

Greg Yedlin, a senator from California, furrowed his brow and stared at Michaels. "I asked if you would address the recent allegations against you that you evaded taxes. And I'd really like a response."

Michaels exhaled and stared off pensively. "I have addressed them. I told you and the rest of the media that they were false, completely fabricated."

"Yet the evidence suggests otherwise."

"I fail to see what this has to do with the issue at

hand," Michaels said. "Senator, I hope you're not simply grandstanding in an effort to gain notoriety and subsequently political clout—because I can assure you that your little plan is backfiring."

"*Pardon* me, sir," Yedlin said. "I wasn't trying to do any of those things. I was simply trying to do my job before you did what you always do. Demean, belittle, disparage—and then you go to great lengths to tell us how smart you are and how we must go along with your little plan no matter what. That's not the kind of leadership we need in this country."

Michaels's eyes narrowed. "And it has nothing to do with the trumped up charges you and your little band of miscreants are investigating, the kind of charges that not even a grand jury would consider. I'm still offended and appalled that you believe I would put my own people in harm's way. I would never do any such thing. Those operatives out there working hard to put an end to terrorists know that is the most ridiculous allegation levied against me. It reveals what the true nature of these hearings are: to get things out in the open so you can rip me down and ride that wave of public sentiment toward regaining power in the senate. You're simply too transparent, Senator Yedlin."

Yedlin adjusted his glasses and stared down at his papers, studying them for a moment before responding.

"I wish we were only under the guise of partisan politics," Yedlin began, "but I'm afraid that just isn't true. We're here because of your gross abuse of power. There are incredible responsibilities required to live in a democratic republic, the least of which is to uphold public trust. And the fact that we've all heard the dramatic tape of you suggesting you were willing to put the men and women who serve this great country in harm's way as a political ploy is beyond revolting. As someone who proudly served in the military—unlike yourself, I might add—I never once questioned whether anything other than the country's best interests were at heart when we received our marching orders. I never once wondered if the only reason I was going somewhere was to prop up a politician's favorability ratings. But I'm saddened by the fact that those serving this great country today *will* now wonder such things."

Michaels took another sip of water and pointed at Yedlin. "Senator, don't be reckless. I think we both know you're just trying to score points with your political base, maybe even bait me into giving you a sound bite that your Super PACs can use in their attack ads when the election cycle begins in earnest. Well, I won't do it. All I will say is that I serve at the pleasure of the American people. I serve them with fervency and diligence. I serve them because I love this country and want to see it kept safe. I serve them because Washington has suffered long enough under the bloated bureaucracy longtime senators such as yourself have created. You and your ilk have been in this city for two or three decades and have produced little substantive change for the American people who so desperately need it. The citizens of this great country are who I serve, and it's a shame I'm wasting my time fighting someone who's supposed to be my ally, not my enemy. But there you sit, trying to score political points like this is a football game. Congratulations, Senator Yedlin, you've simply proven yourself to be another example of Washington's wastefulness. Now, perhaps we can move along so you can stop contributing to global warming with all that hot air you're spouting off."

A low roar erupted from the galley as onlookers discussed the heated exchange between the two men. The head of the committee banged a gavel in an attempt to quiet the conversations.

Michaels looked at Fullbright, who flashed the thumbs up sign. The speech was brilliantly rehearsed, one Michaels had worked on for about a week. He'd memorized every line of it and delivered it with all the passion he felt while writing it. It was all how he felt when he first came to Washington, but even Michaels would admit privately that the city's power was intoxicating. It had consumed him as well, sucked him right into the jetstream like everyone else who'd come to the nation's capital before him.

But the speech sounded good and was guaranteed to resonate with Americans of all stripes and parties. It was all he needed to sway public opinion back in his favor and make everyone forget about the video they'd seen where Michaels *misspoke*. In the political climate of the day, *misspoke* was the excuse *du jour* whenever a politician said something stupid or made a regrettable comment. These poorly worded statements occurred more often, happening mostly due to the proliferation of recording devices. Apologies alone couldn't whitewash such statements. Michaels had learned long ago that the only way to survive in politics was to follow up one's latest *sin* with a win. *Make people forget what they heard and who said it. Remind them why they voted for you in the first place.* And it was a winning formula, time tested and proven over and over again. Michaels had practically turned it into an art form.

So skilled was Michaels that the only thing that ever seemed to stick to him was the nickname Mr. Teflon.

CHAPTER 21

Paris, France

HAWK GENTLY AWOKE ALEX, who'd fallen asleep on his shoulder during their final approach. Though he enjoyed watching her sleep, he needed to talk with her. They didn't have much time to pull off the operation, but success was vital. If Petrov escaped this time, it was anybody's guess as to when she might resurface. And by then, it would likely be too late.

"Get ready," Hawk whispered.

Alex opened her eyes, squinting as she looked around the cabin. "What time is it?"

"Time for us to land," he said.

She sat up in her seat and tightened her seatbelt.

Seconds later, the tires barked as the pilot set the plane down on the runway and then taxied to the executive jet section of Charles De Gaulle Airport. Hawk peered out the window at the blinking lights surrounding the airport and the night skyline serving as a picturesque backdrop. He would've preferred his first trip to Paris with Alex to be under a romantic pretense. But their line of work rarely made room for such indulgences, refusing to guarantee them anything but danger and adventure.

"Isn't this city so beautiful?" she asked, leaning on Hawk's shoulder.

He put his arm around her and pulled her tight. "Maybe we can make another trip here sometime and enjoy Paris for what it is."

"Sounds like a plan."

Once they came to a halt, the team deplaned and went through a watered-down customs process. Their aliases and fake passports withstood the scrutiny of a fastidious customs officer, who defied the norm for even France's open border policy.

After they cleared customs, Blunt sent a man to meet them and brief them on the situation on the ground. Strikingly tall, Ned Villareal shook each person's hand before ushering them toward his vehicle.

"I didn't know Blunt had people working for him in Paris," Samuels said.

Villareal chuckled. "How long have you been working with Senator Blunt? A week? Two?"

"Sounds about right," Samuels said.

"Then you haven't been around him enough to know just how well connected your boss is. He was supposedly dead at one point, but I knew better. No one would take down J.D. Blunt so easily. He might as well be immortal."

"How long have you worked for him?" Hawk asked.

Villareal turned on the blinker as he changed lanes. "For the better part of the past decade, but it's just spot work. Whenever he needs a hand with surveillance or if he wants to confirm a rumor, he contacts me."

"So, who's your actual employer?" Samuels asked.

Villareal smiled and wagged his finger. "Now, that is not a question I will answer under any circumstances, but you're free to make all the suppositions you like. Just don't expect me to confirm or deny any of them."

Hawk shifted in his seat. "So, tell us what we're up against here with Petrov and the rest of The Chamber."

Villareal shrugged. "The usual suspects—tight security, multiple plans, armored body guards, bullet proof convoy vehicles, and an airport checkpoint that will be next to impossible to get into without proper credentials. And weapons? Forget about trying to get them in."

"No weapons?" Hawk asked as he furrowed his brow.

"Don't worry. I've got you covered. The weapons are already safe and sound, hidden at the airport. Getting them out so you can use them is going to be your biggest challenge by far."

Hawk exhaled as he stared out the window at the traffic crawling through the city. "From the way you're talking, it sounds like this operation's only chance is if it were to occur at the airport. Is that correct?"

Villareal nodded. "That's a correct assumption. You have little chance of pulling off any kind of op away from the confines of the airport."

"But we're far more likely to get caught."

Villareal shook his head. "No, you've got it backward, my friend. You're far less likely to get caught in that environment. Too many ways out of the city from there. The checkpoint can easily be evaded."

"How easily?" Samuels asked from the backseat.

"Do you know why there are so many terrorist attacks in France, Mr. Samuels?" Villareal said, not waiting for Samuels to answer. "It's because it's such an easy thing to do. Easy to get in and easy to disappear. It's a nightmare if you're in law enforcement and want to keep tabs on the goings on of your city."

"Then this knife cuts both ways," Hawk said.

"Yes, but it will cut in your favor if you are as good as advertised," Villareal said. "At least, if you're as good as Blunt makes you out to be. He sings your praises as if you were the best agents on the planet."

Hawk nodded confidently. "We're better than advertised then?"

Villareal shot a sideways glance at Hawk. "Even with your rookie back there?"

"That rookie has already saved my life," Hawk said. "I wouldn't call him a rookie any more."

Villareal flashed a quick grin. "Maybe you're the one who's washed up then."

"Maybe, but I'm not quitting until I either get killed or stop Petrov. Those are the only two choices for me."

"You do what you need to do," Villareal said as he drove into a parking deck and went down several stories before pulling into a parking spot. "Let's hustle inside where we can talk more about what you need to do if you intend on stopping Petrov."

CHAPTER 22

New York City

LEE HENDRIDGE HAD BARELY been back in the U.S. for a full day before he was itching to get back to work. His editor, Janet Carlisle, told him to take off all the time he needed. He rested in bed for a day before deciding he needed to head to the office.

As he walked down Eighth Street, Hendridge viewed his pedestrian commute through new eyes. The time he'd spent in the charge of harsh Al Hasib taskmasters induced a type of soul searching he didn't expect. Before he embarked to cover the burgeoning conflict in the Middle East where terrorist groups like Al Hasib were ransacking nearby nations in coordinated attacks, Hendridge saw visions of Pulitzer Prizes dancing in his dreams. When he left, he could only see the death and destruction visited upon a people who were often mischaracterized, even by others who claimed to share the same faith. The children begging in the streets, the rotting stench of death, the oppressive feeling of hopelessness—it all weighed on him, a weight far too great for any one person to bear. And because of that overwhelming sense of despair, Hendridge needed to get to work.

Hendridge needed to do something different for a change, something positive, something that mattered. He no longer aspired to win awards for notoriety's sake—or even to stroke his own ego. He simply wanted his journalism to make a difference in the lives of people. And the people he decided to apply his new outlook on journalism to were Hawk, Alex, and Samuels, the team that saved him when they could've easily left him.

"What are you—?" Carlisle said as she looked up from her morning coffee to see Hendridge standing in her doorway. "I thought I told you to stay home, take the week off, take the month off, take all the—"

"I can't sit still," Hendridge said. "Not any more, not after what happened to me."

She gestured toward the chair across the desk in front of her. "What *did* happen to you out there?"

Hendridge pulled the chair out and sat down. "I don't know if I'm ready to talk about it yet. I mean, it was deeply personal. When I've heard of other people discuss stories of survival in the past, I've shrugged and wondered why people hailed them as heroes, especially when they were getting paid handsomely to share their stories. How much of it was even true at that price? How do we even know if it's real?"

"And now?" she asked, arching her eyebrows.

"It was more real than I knew, more real than I would've ever wanted it to be. The pain was real, both physical and emotional. The abuse was—it was non-stop. The beatings, the mental torture, all of it. I thought I was going insane for a while. And I'd just about given up hope."

"But you didn't, did you?"

"No, I did," Hendridge said. "Except those sneaky little bastards never let me near a sharp object. I'm sure it's because they knew what I would've done had I been left alone with a knife for more than five minutes. I certainly wouldn't be here speaking to you now, that much I know."

"So, how'd you make it?"

"You know those guys wanted for the murder of all those German bankers, the ones in the news?" he asked.

"How'd you know about that?"

He forced a chuckle. "Even terrorists want to read their own press. I also found out they read The Times every day."

"Maybe we can put that in our next advertising campaign," she deadpanned.

"That could be a public relations nightmare, but it is good to know."

"Getting back to what you said earlier, the team of operatives saved you?" Carlisle asked.

"They could've left me for dead, too," Hendridge said. "They were captured by some Al Hasib agents while trying to make a getaway. They almost got me free too but failed."

"And what were you doing during this time?"

"I was just bouncing around like a rag doll," he said. "I had no real purpose, let alone a desire to live. I would've preferred to get left behind at that point, but they refused to leave me alone."

"And here you are."

"It wasn't quite that simple," he said with a smile. "There were many other obstacles to get past in order to make it to this point, but here I am."

"So, what do you want to do about it now? Want to tell your story?"

He nodded imperceptibly. "In time—but for now, I'd like to focus on clearing the names of those agents. I can't believe they did what they're accused of doing. And if they did it, I'm sure there's some reasonable explanation."

"Reasonable explanation for picking off a bunch of leaders of the German banking industry? Perhaps you bumped your head," she said.

He leaned forward in his chair. "Really? That's how you're going to treat me? I'm a damn hero for journalists and you want to make a comment like that?"

"You're not a hero, Hendridge," she said, eyeing him closely. "You're a shill."

"A shill? For who?"

She shrugged. "Does it matter?"

"Hell yeah, it matters. You think I'm making this stuff up."

She bit her lip and thought for a moment. "Let's just say you have a reputation around the newsroom for embellishing. And quite frankly, it wouldn't surprise me if this whole story you're pushing is, shall we say, enhanced."

"Have you lost your mind?" Hendridge said as he stood. "I would never make up anything in print."

"Maybe, but this hasn't gone to print yet. You've never been the subject of intense scrutiny like this story will be sure to bring. If you try to peddle this fiction, plenty of people are going to try and poke holes in it. You'll be found out."

"Do you plan on being one of those people?"

"I plan on vetting this story just like any other. And we're going to need multiple sources to verify it. I'm surely not about to run a first-person piece from you on your alleged kidnapping."

"Alleged? Do you honestly think I would do this to myself?"

She laughed and waved him off. "Nothing your generation does surprises me any more. From the generation who made the vapid Kardashians famous, we have other people who will follow in their footsteps to gain fame, power, or wealth. And in your case, maybe all three."

"If this is a joke, I don't find it very funny. I almost died out there because I was just doing my job. Nobody else wanted this assignment. You only had one taker—and that was me, the only idiot brave enough to venture to the Middle East on this ridiculous assignment."

She rubbed her forehead and picked up her phone, distracted by the vibrating pulses. For a few seconds, she stared at the screen before turning her attention back to Hendridge.

"This assignment wasn't ridiculous. You just weren't the journalist who was capable of pulling it off. You acted like it was some voyeuristic adventure instead of a serious professional assignment. It's why you got caught—and it's why you've returned to try and manufacture some story out of thin air."

"I'm telling you right now that you're wrong," Hendridge said. "These people who saved me are the best of what's right in this world right now, people who fight for justice with integrity and compassion."

"My God, you sound like an Army advertisement. That's not even close to anything I want to print, much less anything our readers would be interested in. Those people are criminals, probably helping you out to assuage their guilty consciences."

Hendridge turned toward the door and stopped as he grabbed the handle, looking back over his shoulder at Carlisle. "You're going to regret this. Everyone will want to know how The Times missed the greatest story of the month when it was right under their noses."

She closed her eyes and shook her head slowly. "Just know when I fire you, no one will touch you or your story."

Hendridge seethed as he exited the office.

I'm going to prove her wrong, even if it's the last story I write.

CHAPTER 23

Paris, France

KATARINA PETROV GREETED Nestor Morozov
with a traditional kiss to the side of each cheek and
welcomed him into her penthouse suite high atop the
city. It would've been considered rude not to treat the
Russian ambassador in such a manner, and she was
never so impolite. As they walked toward the balcony,
the lights winked across the cityscape, giving off the
kind of energy Petrov thrived upon. Something was
happening, and it was well overdue. She'd spent nearly
two decades laboring to guide The Chamber to this
point where the organization could become the
leading entity among a new consortium of nations.
But Petrov never forgot where her true alliances
rested—mother Russia.

She picked up a drink off the table and offered
one to Morozov. He accepted it and thanked her.

"How does it feel to stand on the cusp of greatness?" he asked her.

"I don't know," she said. "How about you tell me?"

Morozov took a long pull on his glass of wine and then set it down on the ledge. "What you've done is truly amazing. Every little detail considered and planned for. You are the master architect behind all of this, and the only genius I consider greater at the moment is the one who put you in charge."

She sighed. "Too bad he won't be around to see his dream realized."

"I'm sure your father is still proud of you, looking down upon all your accomplishments."

Petrov wagged her finger at him. "Don't celebrate just yet. There's still plenty of work to be done."

"Yes, but I see it all coming together—the narrative about the failing wheat crops—"

"While Russia's remains strong."

"And how oil production is falling as uncertainty builds among OPEC nations."

"But production is surging to all-time highs off the Siberian coast."

In a show of admiration, Mozorov shook his head and looked off in the distance before turning his gaze back toward Petrov. "Your patience is something to wonder at. All these years doing what you did—you have embodied the long con."

"It's not difficult when you believe in the cause."

Mozorov chuckled. "So much so that you even married an American."

She shrugged. "He was ruggedly handsome, which made it palatable."

"Yes, well, he also got you pregnant."

"That was my mistake, perhaps the only one."

"But you're still planning on redeeming that *mistake*, aren't you?"

Petrov nodded. "Eventually."

"Has your daughter seen the light?"

She scanned the horizon, remaining pensive for a moment before responding. "She'll come around eventually. Patience, remember?"

CHAPTER 24

Washington, D.C.

PRESIDENT MICHAELS welcomed several members of the national security council into his temporary office and gestured for them to sit at a table in the corner. He shoved a newspaper under his seat. The headline was embarrassing enough, and he didn't want to dwell on the past. The meeting he'd called was all about the future.

"I want to know about the situation with Verge," Michaels said. "Where are we at with that?"

General Isaac Kauffman, the man Michaels had appointed to lead the council, pulled several documents out of his attaché and spread them out on the table. "The details are still trickling in, but it doesn't look like it's as bad as some members of the press previously reported."

Michaels clasped his hands together and shifted

nervously in his seat. "I'd heard oil production might be down for weeks and that millions of barrels of oil would be lost."

"Those are lies, probably issued by OPEC officials to give them a legitimate sounding excuse to boost the price of their product," Kauffman said. "From what I understand, Verge should be back up to full production by the end of today."

"It only took them two days to repair a pipeline blast?"

"Al Hasib didn't sink their teeth in the way they'd hoped."

"How come?"

Kauffman slid a folder across the table to Michaels and remained quiet. Michaels sifted through the pages and slammed his fist down on the table.

"I swear I will take down Brady Hawk myself if I have to," Michaels said.

"Based on your current situation, Mr. President, I'd advise against making that comment again . . . to anyone."

"He's always mucking up my plans and making my life more difficult."

"Perhaps if you hadn't said what you said . . ."

Michaels glared at Kauffman. "Did I hire you to give me your commentary on everything happening within this office? I'll answer that for you since you seem a bit confused right now. The answer is *no*. I hired you to keep me apprised of national security matters and nothing else."

Kauffman nodded sharply. "Understood, sir. I'm just trying to help you see that this situation could've been avoided."

"Again, that's *not* . . . your . . . job."

"In the meantime, Young seems to be covertly using them."

"That's illegal. How is he getting away with that?"

Kauffman shrugged. "Not sure, but he's making an end around somewhere."

"I never thought that bumbling dolt had it in him to do anything worthwhile. It's why I asked him to be my running mate in the first place."

"So, he's your insurance policy?"

"On so many different levels. It's why the senate hearings aren't going to result in any charges against me. No impeachment hearings. No censures. Everyone on Capitol Hill knows we'd be screwed if he permanently sat in the Oval Office. He's a joke."

"At the moment, what he's doing is nothing to laugh at. In fact, while his methods may be suspect—"

"Illegal," Michaels interjected.

"All right, illegal it is, but somehow he's still maneuvering the pieces around the board to hold Al Hasib at bay and thwart one of their biggest attacks in weeks."

"And he's going to pay for his actions. I'll see to that."

Kauffman cleared his throat and pulled back the file he'd given Michaels. "You might want to consider a different approach once you retake command as it relates to national security. Brady Hawk certainly seems to be on your side. I wouldn't view him as an adversary if I were you."

"You're overstepping again, General." Michaels pointed toward the door. "You can show yourself out."

CHAPTER 25

Paris, France

SAMUELS ADJUSTED HIS BOW TIE and then checked his blazer for any remaining strands of lint. He picked off a couple before determining he was clean. Taking a deep breath, he placed his hands on the cart and pushed it down the hall.

"Just stay calm," Hawk said. "Alex and I will be here if you need us. You know what to do."

The operation was simple by any standard, but the importance of what Samuels was doing weighed heavily upon him. To remove the entire leadership of The Chamber in one fell swoop would be a big step in eliminating the clandestine group. While Blunt and the Firestorm team had yet to ascertain the full extent of The Chamber's end game, they knew it was nefarious and detrimental to the U.S. and her allies.

Just breathe, Samuels. You can do this.

The last few weeks had been a blur. Blunt had plucked Samuels out of a job he enjoyed, enticing him by playing to his patriotism. The intrigue of meeting his sister also helped. But Samuels had yet to get to know Alex like he wanted. They might have been related, but it was apparent they came from two different worlds. He considered that maybe that's what it was like for most siblings. It was just an entirely new experience for him. Samuels realized there wasn't much opportunity for conflict in his house as an only child.

He knocked on the door and was met by a pudgy Russian man.

"I have a cart for Ms. Katarina Petrov," Samuels said, reading a card though he didn't need one.

"What is it?"

"A bottle of Krug, Vintage 2002."

The Russian man's eyes widened. "That is her favorite. Who is this from?"

"It's from a gentleman who just checked in downstairs. Would you like me to take it into the room?"

The man shook his head. "I'll take it from here. Thank you." He handed Samuels a note for ten Euros and pulled the cart farther into the room.

"Have a good day, sir," Samuels said before turning and walking away.

He waited until he heard the door click behind him before glancing over his shoulder. Samuels didn't say a word until he was on the elevator.

"Success," he said over his comlink. "Now we wait."

"Good work, *Bro*," Alex said.

"*Bro*? You're ready to move our relationship to that level now, *Sis*?"

Alex laughed. "I always wanted a brother, and now I've got one. I must say I'm still a little surprised I got what I wanted after all these years."

"Be careful what you wish for," Samuels said. "You may not like me making fun of you."

"You may not like me kicking your ass if you try," Alex shot back.

"I'll take that into consideration, *Sis*."

* * *

AN HOUR LATER, ten floors below Petrov, Hawk listened in on the transmission coming from the bug that Alex had hidden beneath the cart. Petrov was discussing plans with the little Russian man who served as her assistant and confidante, Anatoly.

Hawk never could determine if Anatoly and Petrov's relationship went anything beyond the professional realm. Petrov was an attractive woman, especially for her age. But Anatoly was pug faced and balding, even at ten years Petrov's junior. While Hawk hoped to verify the intel they'd received about the plane, he secretly wanted to find out the nagging question of whether there was something more to Petrov and Anatoly.

"Well, Anatoly, it looks like the time has finally arrived," Petrov said.

"Are you sure you want to do this?" he asked.

She was silent for a moment. "Let me ask you a question. If you had the opportunity to seize the throne without any repercussions, would you do it?"

"Depends on what needed to be done to seize it."

"Murder, Anatoly. Cold-blooded murder."

"In that case, I don't think I could."

"Come now. We all have murder in our hearts. There isn't anyone you dream about sliding a knife into their heart and twisting it? There must be someone."

He laughed. "Why would I need to do that when I could simply have you do it for me? Besides, I have much more enjoyable fantasies."

"Such as?"

"You're going to make me blush."

"It wouldn't be the first time," Petrov said. "Now, do tell. I want to hear about your fantasy."

Anatoly was quiet for a moment. Hawk pressed the headphones tighter against his ears, straining to hear what was being said, if anything.

"What is it?" Petrov finally asked.

"It's a message from Bannister."

"Is he still coming?"

"Yes, he said he's been delayed but he'll meet everyone at the airport tomorrow at eight-thirty, just as we'd planned."

"Excellent," she said. "I really liked that man."

"Yet you're still proceeding as planned at the chalet?"

"Of course, Anatoly. Now about that fantasy of yours . . ."

A knock at the door interrupted their conversation again, this time by a hotel employee announcing room service. Everything sounded like it was being consolidated onto one cart, the new cart. The cart Alex had wired was pushed out of the room, transmitting only a squeaky wheel as it rolled out of Petrov's suite and down the hall.

Hawk sighed and put down the headphones.

"So, did you get confirmation?" Alex asked.

Hawk nodded. "Tomorrow night, 8:30."

"Then why do you look so down about it?"

"There was something else they were talking about that I was curious about."

"Care to enlighten me?"

"It was nothing important. Just me being a little voyeuristic, that's all."

Alex eyed him closely. "I never would've pegged you for the type."

"I work in espionage," he said. "What else would you have pegged me for?"

Hawk shifted his weight from one foot to the other, antsy to leave.

"Look, I've got to go out," Hawk said. "I need to meet someone."

"Need me to tag along?" she asked.

"No, you and Samuels bond over your family heritage while you get ready for tomorrow. I can handle this alone, and it's safest that way."

"Suit yourself. Don't hesitate to call me if you need anything."

* * *

HAWK TURNED DOWN THE ALLEYWAY and once again checked the address he'd written down earlier. He was on the right path, though the area felt a little sketchy. Prostitutes had attempted to allure him on every corner, while drug addicts huddled near the doorsteps of back entrances. The smell of urine and sewage almost choked Hawk at times. It was the side of Paris that never appeared on any tourism brochures. It was also a great place for one of the world's best hackers to hide.

Hawk rapped on the door, using the prescribed cadence.

"Name," said a man through an intercom system.

"The Pied Piper," Hawk replied.

Hawk glanced up at the inconspicuous security camera just above the door and waved.

The door buzzed. "Enter," said the man.

Hawk pulled the door open and entered a dimly lit hallway. Waiting a few seconds for his eyes to adjust, he studied the brick walls. He could only guess how long they'd been standing but assumed at least a century or two. Overhead, wooden beams served as high arches, supporting the white roof.

What was this place?

With his vision attuned to the dark environment, Hawk moved forward down the hallway until he reached an open doorway. He stepped inside and found what was likely a banquet hall of some sort. The ceiling soared above as the room sprawled in every direction. Tall windows towered over the hall every few feet but had been covered with a dark material. Hawk studied the chandelier above that used what looked like at least a hundred candles. He was still looking at it when he heard footsteps approaching.

"When you use as much energy as I do for your computer servers, every little bit of savings helps to avoid detection," a man said.

Hawk turned to see a middle-aged man shuffling across the room. He offered his hand to Hawk.

"You must be SnyperNet," Hawk said, shaking the man's hand.

"In the flesh, though I prefer to be called Bob when meeting with people in person."

"And that happens very often?"

"It's only happened once before, but J.D. Blunt is a dear friend of mine."

Hawk nodded. "He must've done something very significant for you."

"He broke my brother out of a Turkish prison, but that's another story for another time. Come. Let's talk."

Bob led Hawk down a hallway and then into a smaller room teeming with electronic equipment. Monitors covered the far wall, while computers were stacked on top of each other on wheeled shelves. A built-in desk ran the length of one wall and had a pair of chairs tucked beneath it. Bob pulled out one of the chairs and gestured for Hawk to sit before joining him.

"The senator tells me you're in a bit of a jam," Bob said, his English accent becoming more pronounced with each sentence.

"That's the understatement of the century," Hawk said. "We'll be going to prison for a very long time if anyone catches us."

"Perhaps I can keep that from happening."

"That's what we're hoping for," Hawk said.

Bob turned toward the keyboard on the desk in

front of him and began typing quickly. "I learned a little bit about your situation from Blunt as well as through news reports, so I started doing a little digging."

"And what did you find?"

Bob tapped out a few more keystrokes before pushing back from the table and staring up at the largest monitor in the room, which was at least eight feet wide and six feet tall. Grainy black-and-white images appeared from a security camera.

"What are we looking at?" Hawk asked.

"Mate, this is the video some powerful person doesn't want anyone to see."

Hawk watched as a person forced masks on the faces of all the German bankers present. His jaw dropped as the footage continued to play.

"It looks like you, doesn't it?" Bob asked.

Hawk nodded. "How the hell did they—?"

"Someone obviously baited you," Bob said. "You were set up from the very first moment. They decided to get rid of two problems at once—the German bankers and then you."

"How could I be in two places at once though?"

"These bastards timed how long it takes to get from one tower to the other. It's about twenty minutes, eighteen if you really hustle."

"And the outside cameras that could prove I never walked that route? Where were they?"

Bob smiled. "There was an outage at that time. Nary a one caught anything during that time. You can't even have an alibi to prove otherwise. It was a perfect op . . . almost."

"Almost?"

"Yes, let's go back to the tape. Do you see the guy who's supposed to be you putting masks on these bankers?"

Hawk nodded. "What of him?"

"Well, I saw a tattoo on his forearm that you don't have."

"And that's proof?"

"Maybe a conspiracy theorist would conjure up some explanation he believed to be plausible, but forensic evidence rarely lies. But just in case that isn't enough, I was able to extrapolate how tall this guy is based on the shadows on the wall. And he's not even anywhere near as tall as you are."

Hawk exhaled but still wore a furrowed brow. "But that doesn't help with the little problem of there being footage of me gunning down these people from my perch on the building next door. I can't deny I did that."

"Yes, but there are ways around this."

"Such as?"

"Leave it to me, but I think I know a way to fix it."

Hawk stood. "When you do, can you send all the video to a journalist I know?" he asked as he held out a business card. "This is how you can get in touch with Lee Hendridge at the *New York Times*. If anyone can take this information and disseminate it to the public, he can—and I know he'll do a good job."

"Was that the journalist whose life you saved?" Bob asked.

Hawk nodded. "We saw him tied up in an Al Hasib camp. I couldn't just leave him there, and the decision nearly got us killed."

"Looks like it'll be the one that might end up saving you, too, so you can get your life back."

Hawk chuckled. "This is my life. Whether I have it back publicly or not makes little difference to me, though the other members of my team might not feel the same way. However, I would appreciate being able to move between countries without being suspected as an assassin."

"Key word there—suspected."

"If you can make this happen, I'll be eternally indebted to you."

Bob waved him off. "I might cash in that favor some day, but in the meantime, don't worry about me. I'll be fine in the dungeon of my own making."

Hawk exited SnyperNet's home and navigated through the dirty streets of Paris. For the first time, he felt like there was hope. The Chamber was on the verge of being fully exposed—and he couldn't wait.

CHAPTER 26

New York City

LEE HENDRIDGE WALKED into Janet Carlisle's office and dropped a typed manuscript on her desk. He crossed his arms and sighed, awaiting her response to his story. But she didn't even pick it up, glancing up at him briefly before returning her attention to something else she was reading.

"Do you have a problem?" Carlisle asked.

"I brought by an article for you to publish," Hendridge said. "I thought you might want to run this in tomorrow's paper."

"Why not just email it to me?" she asked, maintaining her focus on what was in front of her.

"I didn't want you to dismiss it or send it to your junk mailbox," he said. "I wanted to watch you read it."

"I swear you're one relentless little bastard."

"If that's the only disparaging remark you have to make about me today, I'll take it."

Carlisle took her glasses off and then slapped them down on a stack of papers to her right. "Do you see all these, Hendridge?"

He stared past her.

"Look," she said. "I have actual work from actual employees that I need to get to today. I don't have time to read your fantasy pieces when I could be—"

"It's not fantasy, but it's well sourced and is going to make the establishment squeamish at the very least."

"I really don't want to repeat myself." She glanced up and nodded toward the door. "You can show yourself out."

"Come on, Carlisle. Give this article a chance. Don't make a decision until after you've read it. I think you'll be pretty excited."

She rolled her eyes, snatched it off the pile, and skimmed it, slamming one page down after another upon finishing each one. After she completed reading the entire draft, she held it up.

"This is utter garbage," she said. "I can't believe you brought this into my office today. Now go home and get some rest."

"Seriously? There's proof Brady Hawk didn't do what he's accused of doing. It's all getting exposed." He paused. "Or do we not do that any more? Are we simply involved for the money like everyone else at this point?"

She picked up the manuscript and shook it. "Who are your sources for this story?"

"Do you think I'd be willing to risk my journalistic integrity by making this up?" he asked.

"*Who* are your sources?"

"That's the first time I've ever been asked that question by you in five years," he fired back. "You trust me, and you know my work is good. And this story is front page worthy for every newspaper in America and beyond."

"This reads more like a work of fiction to me," she said before slamming it down on her desk.

Hendridge was about to rip into her again, an act that would likely cost him his job, when an uproar in the newsroom grabbed their attention.

"Did you hear?" a reporter asked as she rushed into Carlisle's office. "Michaels has been exonerated. He'll be reinstated as President within the hour."

Carlisle picked up Hendridge's manuscript and dropped it in her trashcan. "Peddle your fiction elsewhere," she said. "Tomorrow we're going to have a real news story on the front page, one that's built upon facts. Maybe you should take some notes."

She got up and exited her office, walking past Hendridge without so much as a glance.

CHAPTER 27

Washington, D.C.

J.D. BLUNT RECOGNIZED the familiar Caller Unknown tag across the top of his phone's screen. He assumed Hawk and the Firestorm team were calling with an update. But Blunt was wrong.

"Did you just hear the news?" a man asked.

It took Blunt a few seconds for the voice to register. Noah Young.

"Did Michaels get cleared?" Blunt asked.

"The committee announced they didn't find any indication of willful wrongdoing and proceeded to recommend he be reinstated in full immediately."

"Well, ain't that just a kick in the pants?" Blunt said, devoid of any emotion.

"This isn't something to joke about," Young said. "I heard Michaels was fuming when he learned Hawk and Samuels were responsible for stopping Al Hasib's attack on the Verge oil facility in Kuwait City."

"He'd get upset if someone shot a charging bull," Blunt countered. "You have to take such reports with a grain of salt. Besides, who told you this?"

"General Kauffman."

"Kauffman."

"Yeah, apparently the General kept meeting with Michaels to keep him abreast of what was going on in the event that he got reinstated soon. I guess it was just a precautionary measure."

"Bullshit. Michaels is up to something. He should've never been briefed under the circumstances of the agreement."

"Well, he knows I've been talking to you apparently, that I was the one who informed Hawk and the team about the potential attack."

Blunt huffed softly through his nose. "And who told him that? Frank Stone?"

"Maybe, but my money is on Kauffman."

"Why would Kauffman do that to us? He was supposed to be our ally in all of this."

"Just goes to show you can't trust anyone in this town."

Blunt sighed. "That doesn't show me anything. I've known that for years, but that doesn't mean I'm still not surprised sometimes when people switch allegiances and what motivates them to do so."

"So, what's our next move?" Young asked, the angst in his voice elevating.

"Stay calm and don't breathe a word of this to anyone else, understand?"

"Got it," Young said. "Is there anything I can do to help? I really want to help."

"Stay out of the way," Blunt said. "That's always the best way for you to assist me in this process. Leave it in the hands of the professionals and move forward."

Blunt hung up and sauntered over to his record player. He sifted through several jazz albums before he found one he felt fit his mood. Charles Mingus, *Better Git It In Your Soul.* He inspected the vinyl before putting it on and pouring himself a glass of scotch.

Blunt needed to think. He needed to figure out a way to avoid becoming a target of Michaels. Blunt needed to put the bullseye back where it belonged— on the President of the United States.

CHAPTER 28

Paris, France

PETROV STEPPED INTO THE STRETCH limousine first at the behest of her guests. She wasn't sure if it was a sign of respect, chivalry, or distrust. Ultimately, she didn't care. Tucked out of sight up her right thigh was a holster for her gun. She felt it just to make sure it was still there. Eventually, she'd have to use it, but not now. Not here. No, she intended to make her point with more than a simple bang. She had much more in mind for each of The Chamber's board members.

Ricardo Valencia, the Mexican ambassador to Russia, slipped into the seat next to Petrov. She considered him a valuable asset based on his connections to the Western hemisphere. But, like everyone else climbing into the limo with her, he was still expendable.

Once the final passenger was loaded, bringing the total number to seven, the driver shut the door and then drove them toward the airport. Outside, the lights of Paris flickered against the twilight. A discussion broke out about the best restaurant in the city, quickly followed by a robust debate over the finest wine. Petrov remained quiet amid both conversations.

"Katarina," Valencia began, "what is it that keeps you so preoccupied tonight? You seem distant."

"I apologize, Ricard," she said. "I'm lost in my thoughts about The Chamber."

"And what might those thoughts be?" he asked. "I'm sure everyone here would be interested to hear them."

She took a deep breath and exhaled slowly. "I'm excited—but nervous—about what's happening with The Chamber."

"Nervous? You?" Ricardo asked, resulting in soft chuckling among the rest of the contingent.

"I know it's difficult to believe, isn't it?" she said, forcing a smile. "But the truth is I see The Chamber changing the world."

Richardo nodded. "I think we all believe that in some form or another or else we wouldn't be here."

Petrov held up her hands. "No, not like that. Not in the way that most people make such statements in an offhanded way. When I say *change the world*, I'm talking about a real and practical manner. In fact, I actually mean it."

"What does that look like to you?" Ricardo asked.

Petrov glanced out the window for a moment and rubbed the corners of her eyes, trying to contain her emotions.

"When I was a little girl growing up in St. Petersburg—it was called Leningrad at that time—all I wanted was peace," she began. "Perhaps it's because I was surrounded by such violence. I only had to step outside my flat to see people getting pummeled for breaking some sort of arbitrary law. And it was no better inside either."

She sighed before continuing. "My mother—she was a bit of a pushover. I wanted a stronger mother. In fact, it's what I prayed for every night back when I believed that God existed and that he cared about me. But I no longer believe in such fanciful and whimsical things, perhaps to my detriment. Only time will tell."

She thought for a moment then proceeded with her story.

"My mother only grew weaker and weaker, beaten down by life. She was also beaten down by my father—every . . . single . . . night. He would come home from one of his vodka-fueled drunken excursions and beat my mother. I begged her to stand up to him, to fight for herself, to fight for me. But she wouldn't. She would just take it, night after night. To be honest, I don't know if there was an exact point where my father damaged her beyond repair, but it happened. One night I watched her cover her head with her arms and writhe about on the floor while my father kicked her and punched her like she was a thief he was arresting. That night as she moaned in the hallway, I vowed while lying in my bed that I would never become like her, so weak, so powerless, so unwilling to fight back."

She exhaled and then took another deep breath, her voice starting to quake.

"The next morning, I went into her room and stared at the bruises. Her eyes were almost swollen shut. Her nightgown was ripped, and I could see huge contusions everywhere. And while I wanted to have pity for her, I couldn't. She was a stout woman and could've stood up to him, but she chose to just lie on the floor and let him treat her like a dog. So I found the only pity I had in my heart for her, which gave me the strength to put a pillow over her face and suffocate her. It took about a minute, one long, excruciating minute that ticked past, each second full of more regret than the last. But it was never enough to make me stop. I couldn't stop. I wouldn't stop until she was out of her misery."

She looked up at The Chamber board members, all of them eyeing her cautiously. While they were all ruthless in their endeavors, Petrov knew none of them were cold hearted enough to kill their own mothers. She planted a seed of doubt in their heads, though they'd never do anything about it. Too many of them already saw her as an ally, as a friend. And she wanted it that way. Gain their trust and their empathy, and then seize what you want. That was the Petrov way, the way her father taught her, the way the academy taught when she enrolled after killing her mother.

"I didn't go to her funeral," Petrov continued. "I felt as though it would've been hypocritical to do such a thing. Seeing her lying peacefully after I killed her—that was the first time I'd ever seen her like that. Fully at peace was how I longed to see her. And I finally saw her reach that state. But it changed me, for the better of course. It made me realize what I wanted to do with my life: I wanted to fight bullies by becoming one."

Petrov took the calculated risk that *bully* had not yet become a nasty four-letter word among her traveling companions. And she was right. They nodded in agreement, each person understanding what she meant. Perhaps her story didn't scare them, but it sure made them think.

"That's what we do at The Chamber," Petrov

added. "We stand up to bullies, no matter who they are."

Ricardo leaned forward and grabbed several glasses from the minibar in the back, doling them out one by one. He removed a chilled glass of champagne from a bucket of ice and passed it around. When everyone had a full glass, he raised his in the air.

"I propose a toast," he began, "to Katarina Petrov, the woman who will stand with you in the face of injustice no matter what. I wouldn't want anyone else standing by my side in times such as these."

Calls of "here, here" echoed throughout the limousine, followed by the clinking of glasses.

"We will rise," Petrov said, her steely gaze scanning all the passengers seated around her. "The Chamber will rise."

She took a swig from her glass and drained it before sliding her hand along the upper part of her right thigh. Her gun was still there, and she was itching to use it.

CHAPTER 29

HAWK PRESSED THE BINOCULARS close against his face as he surveyed the approaching vehicle. The private section of Charles De Gaulle operated by different rules, rules that made it easy to flaunt security measures. On the way to the airport, Hawk and Alex had received an earful from Samuels, who derided such practices for the executive flight club. He railed about how the rich lived by another set of standards. Hawk refused to disagree, mostly because Samuels had a sound argument, but also because it was clear he was like a dog with a chew toy when it came to lecturing about protocol and what was fair.

"What do you see, Hawk?" Samuels asked over his coms.

"I see Petrov getting out of the limo," Hawk answered. "She's carrying a weapon."

Hawk smiled and waited for the predictable response.

"That burns me up that someone like her could just walk in here with a gun," Samuels said. "What's to stop her from strolling into the terminal and shooting people at will?"

"I believe she has other plans tonight," Hawk said. "And we're going to disrupt them."

"It makes me so mad," Samuels said.

"Settle down, Bro," Alex said. "We'll take care of her soon enough."

"That won't change a thing," Samuels said. "There will still be—"

"Put a sock in it, Samuels," Hawk said sternly. "We're done discussing the privilege of the wealthy. It's a fact of life. Time for you to move on."

Hawk took a deep breath to settle his nerves and identified the rest of the party traveling with Petrov.

"Did you get all that?" Hawk asked after he finished.

"Copy that," Alex said. "Now, go set that bird up."

"My pleasure."

Hawk put on a cap and drove the catering truck toward the plane. He watched the captain greeting his passengers, glancing nervously at his watch between interactions.

Once Hawk pulled the truck to a stop near the rear of the plane, he hustled across the tarmac to meet the pilot and put on his glasses.

"Sorry I'm late," Hawk said in French. "I got held up at a security checkpoint."

"Make it quick," the French pilot answered. "We need to get out of here as soon as possible."

Hawk nodded and ran back to his truck where he began unloading the food trays, taking them up the steps, and delivering them to the plane's galley. He could've finished his job in one trip, but he held some back so he could wait for the pilot to climb aboard.

Hawk smiled at the flight attendant who responded by giving him a tongue lashing. He didn't understand half of what she said, but he didn't need to because the message was clear: She was upset. He felt a moment of pity for her as she'd soon become a casualty of war. She was innocent, after all, though he could never be too sure.

"Are you getting all this?" Hawk asked.

"Every second of it," Alex responded over the coms. "Those glasses are amazing. I'm running everyone through facial recognition now as we speak."

"Hopefully with better results than last time," Hawk said as he slid the last food trays out of the truck.

"Yes, the resolution is much clearer," she said.

Alex then chuckled.

"What is it?" Hawk asked.

"You'll get a kick out of this. That flight

attendant who was so mean to you is actually a Mexican assassin."

"Does she have ties to Petrov?"

"Not according to what I'm reading here," Alex said.

"Well, that's bizarre."

"Yeah, and now you don't have to feel bad about what you're going to do."

Hawk shook his head and sighed. "Who said I felt bad?"

"I've known you long enough, Hawk. It's probably written all over your face."

He delivered the last food trays and saluted the captain standing at the back. The captain gave Hawk a half-hearted wave that looked more like a shooing motion than a friendly adieu.

Hawk raced down the steps and quickly stuck the two explosive charges to each wing before dashing back to his truck. He jumped into the driver's seat and roared down the tarmac.

One of the caterers who'd been bound and gagged before Hawk knocked him out stirred in the back of the truck. It was just enough of a distraction that Hawk didn't see Petrov slip off the plane.

CHAPTER 30

PETROV CHEWED HER FINGERNAILS while she awaited the plane to finish loading. Her mission was a simple one: kill the entire board of The Chamber. It was the only way to take full control and help realize the vision her father had set out for the organization once the Iron Curtain fell. But as she glanced out the window, she saw something that made her even more nervous.

The man who'd delivered the food to the plane reminded her of someone. Maybe it was his muscular build or the way he carried himself, but he seemed out of place as a caterer. She just couldn't quite place him.

But when she saw him dash beneath the plane, she knew. It was Brady Hawk.

Petrov faked a phone call and claimed it was imperative that she deplane. She promised to meet them all at the private chalet in the Swiss Alps. The board members all appeared worried, not for their own safety, but for her wellbeing.

"Are you sure you don't want me to stay behind with you?" Ricardo asked.

"No," she said as she stepped outside at the top of the platform. "I'll be fine. Anatoly is coming for me. I'll just charter another plane and meet you there in the morning. This can't really wait."

Ricardo nodded. "I understand. But still, if you want me to stay with you—"

She waved him off. "No, Ricardo. You go and have a good time with the others without me. This is personal, and I don't want to involve you in my personal affairs."

"Very well," he said before kissing her on each side of her cheek.

Petrov forced a smile and then turned her back to walk down the steps. She knew she'd never see him again. However, she wasn't too distraught over that fact. If Brady Hawk hadn't intervened, she would've done the task herself. But dying herself? That wasn't part of Petrov's plan.

She glanced back at the plane once more and quickly spotted the two explosive devices beneath each wing.

That's how I would've done it. She admired Brady Hawk just as much as she wanted to kill him.

She wobbled in her heels as she headed toward the private executive jet lounge set just off the tarmac.

Taking a seat at the bar, she ordered a martini and lit another cigarette moments after crushing the butt of her previous one.

A well-dressed man sat next to her and flashed a smile. He ordered a drink and struck up a conversation.

"Where are you headed?" the man asked.

"Far away from here," she said, trying to resist the urge to engage with him.

"What kind of jet do you have?"

"The best," she said before a fireball lit up the night sky, interrupting their fledgling conversation.

The man hustled over to the door along with a small throng of people. Petrov watched as they all went slack-jawed, shaking their heads in disbelief. She returned to her drink and played with the toothpick, olive still attached.

"Can you believe that?" the man asked as he sat back down next to her.

Petrov shrugged. "The world isn't what it used to be."

"Perhaps, but I've never seen anything quite as spectacular as that."

"A giant fireball in the sky?" she said, casting a sideways glance at him. "You need to get out more."

"I wholeheartedly agree. Now, where were we— oh, yes, you were telling me about your jet."

Petrov ignored the line of questioning regarding her plane for a couple reasons. For starters, she couldn't remember what type it was. And she concluded if she could recall the make and model, it might somehow indict her since that was the same type of plane that just exploded over Paris. Instead, she launched into a story that she fabricated on the spot about her life as a billionaire heiress. For twenty minutes, she regaled him with tales of adventure on her father's yacht, sky diving over Maldives, surfing near the Great Barrier Reef, and navigating a small barge along the Amazon.

"Sounds like you're a modern-day Richard Halliburton," the man said.

She smiled. "I'll take that as a compliment, though I've yet to swim the Panama Canal like he did."

"You're still young," he said before getting up and tossing some cash on the bar. "Hopefully I'll see you again."

Petrov exhaled as he left. She was glad he was gone, but she couldn't deny that she enjoyed the attention. A dashing man in his late 30s flirting with her—there were worse ways to pass the time while awaiting Anatoly to pick her up.

The televisions behind the bars all cut away from a live soccer match to a report about the plane crash. Reporters were already on the scene, describing the "fireball in the sky" that killed a reported seven passengers and three crew members.

Six passengers, thankfully.

Petrov realized her escape had little to do with her intuition and everything to do with a stroke of luck. It took both clairvoyance and fortune to survive in her world. She smiled at the thought of Brady Hawk and his team celebrating her early demise. However, they were unaware that she escaped, giving her an upper hand she hadn't held in quite some time.

I couldn't have planned this any better myself.

CHAPTER 31

HAWK WAS DRIVING BACK toward the hotel when the devices detonated. He pulled off to the shoulder and watched as the fiery debris fell to the ground. Some of the pieces sped rapidly downward while others drifted. A dark plume of smoke rose from the spot where the bulk of the hull landed.

He exhaled in relief. He'd done it. After trying for so long to put an end to The Chamber, it was now in shambles, nothing more than a pile of ashes sitting on a tarmac. However, the rest of the Firestorm team didn't share his enthusiasm.

When Hawk walked into the room, he was greeted by two pensive faces.

"I thought you guys would be more excited," Hawk said as he locked the door behind him. "This feels more like I just walked in on a funeral."

Alex shook her head and sighed. "In a way it is. My mother is dead."

"She was dead to you a long time ago, Alex. Don't try to—"

"Stop," she said, holding up her hand. "Just stop. There were still things I wanted to ask her, things I wanted to know about my life growing up—like if she ever really loved me or if I was just part of her assignment. Now, I'll never know."

"Hey, look," Hawk said as he tried to put his arm around her.

She brushed him off. "I just need some time and space, Hawk. It's nothing personal."

Hawk turned toward Samuels, who was seated at the kitchen table. "And what's your reason for the long face?"

Samuels shook his head. "I don't know. I've just got a feeling about this."

"What kind of feeling?"

"The kind that gets a hold of you and won't let go."

Hawk sat at the table across from Samuels. "And what is this feeling telling you?"

"I'm not going to celebrate this as a success until I see Petrov's dead body."

Hawk laughed nervously. "You think she survived a blast like that? The device was set to blow once the jet reached five hundred feet. Do you honestly think she'd still be alive if she fell from that distance, let alone avoid getting burned up in the explosion?"

"Hey," Alex said, "do you need to be so graphic?"

Hawk turned back toward Samuels. "If you're feeling this way, you must have a theory about how she could've made it out alive."

"I can't explain it right now, but we need to see her body to verify the mission is complete."

Hawk's eyes widened. "You do realize that showing up at the scene of the crime crawling with law enforcement would be breaking protocol, right? Not to mention stupid since the last I heard Interpol was still hunting for us."

"Screw protocol," Samuels said. "This is different."

Hawk grinned. "You're coming around, Samuels. You're starting to think like a real operative."

Samuels glared at Hawk. "I didn't say *I* wanted to be the one to inspect the bodies."

Hawk shook his head and rolled his eyes. "Figures. But I'll do."

* * *

ALEX FABRICATED CREDENTIALS for Hawk, while Samuels helped Hawk create a disguise. They decided he'd pose as a Gulf Stream executive based out of Paris. He would claim the corporate office made a special request for him to visit the active investigation scene to look for intricacies about the engine that the French police might miss. Hawk knew that in situations like this, timing mattered because the FAA likely already had someone on a plane to Paris. And the presence of any true officials would complicate things.

"Think you can pull this off?" Alex asked as she handed Hawk his employee identification badge along with a small stack of business cards.

"I always think I can pull everything off," he said.

"And sometimes you don't."

"True, but this won't be one of those times."

Hawk returned to the airport with Alex and Samuels in tow. The latter pair remained in their vehicle, while Hawk hustled across the tarmac toward the smoldering plane. Working with airport security, French police had already set up a bank of lights to assist with the immediate investigation. A small group of reporters crowded near the tape cordoning off the scene. One officer was stationed there, tasked with ensuring they didn't get any closer.

Toting a briefcase, Hawk walked briskly toward the tape before lifting it up. He continued closer as if he belonged. The officer flagged him down before Hawk stopped.

"What are you doing?" the French officer asked.

"This is an active investigation scene. You are not allowed in there."

Hawk held up his credentials. "I work for the company who makes these jets, and they asked me to inspect the aircraft to see if I can detect any abnormalities ahead of the FAA's arrival in the morning."

The officer shined his flashlight on the identification card. "I'll need to clear this with my commander."

Hawk eyed him closely. "Are you sure you want to bother him with such a request? This is standard protocol. How many plane crash scenes have you worked?"

The officer shook his head and waved Hawk through. "Fine. Go ahead."

"Thank you, sir."

Hawk walked toward the scene where he was met by several French officials.

"Who are you, and who let you in here? This area is restricted," one of the men said.

"I'm Gabriel Laurent with Gulfstream," Hawk said, pulling off his best French accent. "I'm here to inspect the crash scene for liability purposes."

"Do not touch anything."

"I won't."

Hawk walked around the crash site, observing

and taking notes. However, all he was really concerned with were the bodies. After walking the perimeter, he saw them lined up on a white sheet off to the side. He strolled over to the area where an officer was tagging each one.

"You recovered the ten bodies already?" Hawk asked.

"Nine," the officer said.

"I thought the news said ten."

"I think the manifest with the charter company listed ten, but we've only been able to recover nine."

"Is it a male or female missing?" Hawk asked. "It matters for liability purposes."

"Female," the officer answered. "Who are you again?"

"Thank you for your time."

Hawk had already noticed the only pair of women's feet sticking out from beneath the sheet. Despite their mangled condition, he could still identify which toes had spent time being pedicured and which ones hadn't. And the only pair that had been handled with care didn't have Petrov's distinct ankle tattoo. The officer only confirmed what he'd already suspected.

"She wasn't on that plane," Hawk said over his com as his gait picked up while leaving the scene.

"What?" Alex asked in bewilderment. "When did she—?"

"I don't know how or when she exited the plane," Hawk said. "I don't think she saw me. I was really careful. But maybe she did. Or maybe she set us up again."

"No," Samuels said. "No way. Something had to have spooked her, and she decided to get off that plane before takeoff."

"It was probably me then," Hawk said.

He was so engrossed in the conversation that he hadn't heard the men calling after him until now.

"What's going on?" Samuels said. "Sounds like something's happening."

Hawk glanced over his shoulder. "Shit. I think I've been made."

He looked back, this time to notice two officers sprinting toward him.

"Alex, have the car ready. We need to disappear— and fast."

CHAPTER 32

Kuwait City, Kuwait

KARIF FAZIL LOOKED at his watch and waited. The intel several of his men gathered over the past week documented the exact times at which Verge's security detail changed shifts. It was the moment when the oil refinery was most vulnerable. It was the time when Fazil would strike.

He squeezed the steering wheel and took a deep breath. He didn't like getting so involved in operations that he put himself in harm's way. Preferring to call the shots from afar, he concluded that with his well-trained soldiers, his presence was rarely necessitated. But the number of those loyal to him had dwindled, mostly due to the devastating drone attack a few nights prior. What was supposed to be a celebration turned into a blood bath.

The Americans.

Fazil spit out of the window in disgust. Their plans to bring Verge to its knees had been spoiled by Brady Hawk and his team. Fazil, who'd been monitoring the attack from Morocco, assembled the flight crew for his private jet once he learned his men captured Hawk. But by the time Fazil landed and reached the camp, another development had superseded the American agent's capture. Al Hasib's camp location on Failaka Island had been given away and quickly became the target of a strike. It decimated Al Hasib's troops as less than a dozen of the fifty men running the operation managed to survive and escape.

This is for every one of my loyal men.

Fazil glanced at his watch and then back at the gate to Verge. The guards were changing as scheduled.

He smiled and turned the ignition, firing up the truck. Stomping on the gas, the truck lurched forward and sped toward the gate.

"What do they say in America? 'If you want it done right, you have to do it yourself?'" he said aloud. He followed that with a guttural scream.

The truck ripped through an access arm and rumbled over a spike strip. With the tires wobbling, Fazil held the steering wheel steady as he neared his intended target. Guards scrambling outside fired off bullets that whizzed past the truck and peppered the windshield. Hunching low in the cab, Fazil dragged a cinder block onto the accelerator and prepared to make his escape by scooting to the passenger side.

He counted down as he neared one of the towers.

Three . . . two . . . one . . .

He swung the passenger door open and dove head first onto the ground. Flailing about for twenty meters, he finally came to a stop, just in time to see his truck slam into a tower and set off a fiery explosion that spewed oil into the air.

Fazil clambered to his feet and hustled toward the exit. Security personnel were too busy gawking at the flaming refinery to even notice the terrorist stealthily escaping through the main gate. One of Fazil's men was waiting for his boss less than a hundred meters from the entrance. Fazil hopped inside.

"Let's go," Fazil said.

The vehicle left without a single Verge security SUV following in pursuit.

"Take that, Brady Hawk!" Fazil said before breaking into loud, nervous laughter.

CHAPTER 33

Paris, France

BY THE TIME HAWK SAW the escape vehicle, sirens were already blaring in the distance. He managed to extend the gap between himself from the two officers in pursuit, but that wasn't going to stop them. If they caught up with Hawk and his team, French officials would quickly learn that they were the same group accused of the Stuttgart Massacre, the moniker coined by the European press.

"You two should go ahead and let me sort this out on my own," Hawk said over his com as he ran.

"We're a team," Alex said. "We're sticking together."

"Leaving you behind would go against protocol," Samuels said.

"You and that damn protocol," Hawk said. "It's going to get you killed one day."

"Today, it's saving your ass," Samuels fired back. "Now hurry up."

Hawk tried to suck in more air as he pumped his arms and raced toward Alex and Samuels. With legs burning and chest aching, Hawk powered on, ignoring the pain. Less than a minute later, he approached the SUV.

"Samuels, you better not be in the driver's seat," Hawk said.

"She's all yours," Samuels said. "Getting in the backseat now."

Hawk slipped behind the wheel and already had his foot on the accelerator before the door was shut. The engine whined and roared as they flew out of the parking lot.

"You know," Hawk said, "I knew this was a stupid idea."

Alex huffed a soft laugh through her nose. "That's rich coming from you. Have you kept track of all your stupid ideas? Because I have, and you've acted on at least two dozen of them."

Hawk shook his head slowly. "One man's stupid idea is another man's genius."

"Well, we found out the truth, didn't we?" Samuels chimed in.

"It would've eventually come out," Hawk said, checking his rearview mirror.

"But by then, Petrov would've had a huge head start and may have disappeared," Samuels argued. "Charles de Gaulle has temporarily halted all departures, so at least we know she's still in the city."

"A lot of good that's going to do us if we're sitting in a Paris jail somewhere."

Hawk turned a corner and saw several police cars heading toward them about 400 meters down the road.

"I'm gonna need some help navigating here, Alex," Hawk said.

She typed furiously on her laptop. "Take the next right."

Hawk whipped the vehicle to the right, tires screeching as he turned. He bumped along a narrow street until he approached another major intersection.

"Which way?"

"Left."

Hawk followed her instructions before she led them down another small alleyway off the main road. When Hawk saw an open garage, he darted inside.

"You sure this is a good idea?" Alex asked.

Hawk nodded. "This is how we lose them. They're not going to find us in here."

"We need to split up," Samuels said. "But we need a new rendezvous point. They'll be watching for us at the hotel."

"Memorize this address," Hawk said before giving them the address of SnyperNet. "The passcode is the Pied Piper, okay? Don't forget it. He won't let you in under any circumstances."

Samuels and Alex nodded.

"Be careful, both of you," Hawk said.

Before they had time to respond, a convoy of police cars roared into the parking garage.

All three of the fugitives scrambled to get out of view of the headlights, but one of the police vehicles came to a stop just behind the SUV. Officers spilled out of the cars.

Hawk held his hands up and stood gingerly. "I surrender," he said.

One of the officers rushed over and roughly handcuffed Hawk.

"How did you find us?" Hawk asked.

The apparent officer in charge smiled. "Never underestimate the power of French CCTV." He gestured toward Samuels and Alex who were crouching nearby. "Arrest them, too."

"You might want to see this," one of the officers said, handing his superior a tablet.

"Well, what do you know? It's the three criminals responsible for the Stuttgart Massacre. You just made my night, maybe even my career."

CHAPTER 34

Thurmont, Maryland

BLUNT LOATHED NAVIGATING the quagmire of Washington traffic. However, he enjoyed a short road trip, the kind where he didn't have to worry with clogged city arteries or depend on the faulty navigational app on his phone. He just wanted to drive and think.

After a tumultuous few days, he needed a respite from the chaos, even if he knew it would only be brief. The breaking story that the trio responsible for the Stuttgart Massacre had been nabbed by French Police the day before made Blunt's stomach churn. He wanted to think about anything else but struggled to do so. However, he thought Noah Young's request that Blunt make the jaunt north of Washington to Camp David might help get his mind off the mess in Paris. But Young had a predicament of his own. Since

Michaels's reinstatement, Young had been reluctant to meet with his superior.

While Young remained confident that Michaels couldn't legally do anything to him, the president would certainly attempt to freeze Young out and neuter him at best, vengefully destroy his allies at worst. Young prepared for the worst.

Blunt had been a longtime confidante of Young, dating back to their time together at Princeton. Neither of them ever expected to be where they were in terms of power and influence, but it wasn't a shock to anyone who knew both men. They were cut from the same cloth—driven, determined, dedicated. Most importantly, they were fiercely loyal, both to each other and their country. And during the time since Michaels's return to power, both expressed fear for the other.

After several checkpoints, Blunt cleared security and arrived at the main lodge. When he pulled up, Young was waiting outside.

"It's good to see you," Young said as he shook Blunt's hand. The exchange quickly turned into a hearty hug.

"You too," Blunt said, glancing around at the Marines on duty. "Let's get inside somewhere so we can talk."

Young led Blunt to a great room overlooking the

grounds. The trees were green and full, swaying gently in the early morning summer breeze. Squirrels scurried back and forth between towering oaks. Birds chirped a constant calm refrain. For Blunt, the nature scene stood in stark contrast to the roiling storm brewing in Michaels's wake just sixty miles south of them.

"I didn't know if you'd be able to make it with the way things have been lately," Young said.

"I'll drop anything to help you," Blunt said. "You know that."

"Your team needs you," Young said. "And they need you because I asked them to take on an assignment."

"That's what Firestorm is all about. Hawk, Alex, Samuels—none of them would accept your apology even if you gave them one."

Young shrugged. "That might be how you feel, but I still feel the weight of each decision."

"That burden has been lifted now."

Young cast a sideways glance at Blunt. "I'm not happy about it. He's coming for me, J.D."

"He's coming for all of us."

"In the meantime, I want to know how I can help your team. They're in a tough spot."

"You can't," Blunt said. "Nobody can. We're all stuck here. Hawk knew they would be on their own yet took the assignment anyway."

Young paced around the room. "Aren't there any favors you can call in with the French?"

"It's not the French who hold the power here. It's Interpol. And I don't exactly have many friends over there."

Young's eyebrows shot upward. "Oh?"

Blunt waved him off. "It's a long story and not one I want to get into right now. It's involves lots of cheap booze, women, and some serious indiscretions while in Berlin once."

"Say no more," Young said. "Look, I only want to help. You insist that this is their job, but I can't help but think how I'm responsible. If I hadn't sent them . . ."

"It was only a matter of time before they got caught, either stateside or there."

"At least they would've had a fighting chance here."

Blunt sighed and shook his head. "What they really need is for someone to exonerate them." He took out a cigar and started gnawing on it.

"Still chewing on those things?" Young asked.

"Only when I'm nervous—or not."

Young chuckled. "So, how are we going to clear their names? We know Petrov set them up with those German bankers."

"They met with a guy I know who specializes in

those things, but I'm not sure if they got anywhere with him. We haven't exactly had hours to debrief, if we've had any contact at all."

A knock at the door interrupted their conversation.

"Pardon the interruption, sir," a Marine said as he stepped inside the room. "The president is on line one for you."

Young ambled over to the desk in the corner of the room and picked up the receiver before pressing 1 on the console and putting the call on speaker.

"Good morning, Mr. President," Young said.

"I bet you never thought you'd say that to me again, did you, you little rat?" Michaels said. "I just wanted to warn you that I'm coming for you. I'm going to make you a lame duck vice president if there ever was one. You're going to wish you never joined me on the ticket."

"Too late for that," Young said.

"Your little secret agent friends are getting exactly what they deserve—and you will too soon enough."

Young's eyes widened as he looked at Blunt, who reassured his friend with a gesture that shrugged off the threat. Before Young could respond, the line went dead.

"Damn it," Young said. "We're screwed."

Blunt took a deep breath and exhaled slowly. "I

wouldn't count Hawk out yet, but you, on the other hand, have an uphill battle to fight. You're the one who's going to need more help than anyone as you butt heads with the most powerful man in the world."

"You really think you can help me?" Young asked.

"Sure," Blunt said.

No harm in telling a lie.

CHAPTER 35

New York City

LEE HENDRIDGE TAPPED HIS PENCIL against the arm of the chair while waiting for Janet Carlisle to finish reading his piece. Only two days before, Hendridge received a video showing how someone made the German bankers from the Stuttgart Massacre appear to look like certain powerful leaders with ties to The Chamber, a secret organization that national security officials labeled as terroristic in nature. Most of Hendridge's report was working off deep background and an unlikely casual interview of the trio accused of the crime.

Carlisle remained resistant to the story idea but eventually caved. When Hendridge showed her the video along with two corroborating video forensic experts verifying the authenticity of the images, she considered it. Yet Hendridge's threat to quit and take his story to *The Daily News* persuaded her to relent.

"Who is The Chamber?" she asked. "I've never heard of this group."

"They operate in the shadows, influencing prominent people, both in the private sector and government," Hendridge said. "Not much is known about them, at least not the kind of information any of my contacts at Homeland Security were willing to divulge. The general consensus seems to be that they're dangerous—and so is anyone who works with them."

"Who's their leader?" Carlisle asked.

Hendridge shrugged. "Nobody knows, or at least no one would tell me. I did a lot of digging into them but couldn't find a thing about them anywhere."

"But your bandit friends know about them?"

He nodded. "They didn't say it outright, but that's why they were there. They got a tip that they could eliminate these leaders and went for it."

"If you could enhance the video footage, maybe you could identify who the people were supposed to be by the masks they were wearing," Carlisle suggested.

"That's what I thought too, but the video experts I spoke to said they couldn't enhance the images any more."

"So, this is as good as it gets?" Carlisle asked, gesturing toward the article print out on her desk.

"For now," Hendridge said. "But I can keep digging with some follow up stories. The important thing is that this article could get them all released."

"And you're sure these are the same three being held in Paris? No media outlet has mentioned the names of the agents arrested. I haven't even seen their names on any conspiracy websites."

Hendridge cocked his head to one side. "You read conspiracy websites?"

She ignored him. "The point is you might be doing some killers a favor if this isn't them."

"It's them," he said. "I know it. I got one State Department official to tell me off the record the name of one of the agents arrested. They're not even willing to help them at this point."

"Fine," she said. "I'll post it this afternoon. If this story is really as big as I think it's going to be, I definitely don't want this to get lost in the Michaels's coverage."

Hendridge exhaled and smiled. "I promise you're making the right call here." He turned toward the door.

"Hendridge," she began, "don't ever threaten me to take a story to *The Daily News* again because I'll let you go to that rag in a heartbeat next time."

Hendridge smiled sheepishly. "You know they'd have a better headline than us on this story."

She shook her head. "Get outta here, and start working on a follow up for tomorrow."

* * *

WHEN NEWS BROKE in *The New York Times* about how secret operatives were targeting known terrorists in the bait and switch by the leader of an unnamed clandestine terrorist organization known as The Chamber, Washington was abuzz. Other media pounced on the story, while government officials worked to identify the three Interpol had arrested.

Blunt celebrated the news by pouring himself a glass of scotch far earlier in the day than usual and calling the head of Interpol, Jinjing Bao, a former Chinese UN ambassador who managed to ascend to the top of the law enforcement alliance of nearly 200 countries. Blunt had spent time with Bao in the past while drawing up trade legislation that affected the United States' relationship with China. While considering Bao a friend was a long stretch, Blunt knew the Interpol leader would take his call and have a conversation.

"What a pleasure to speak with you, Senator Blunt," Bao said, "though not surprising given the nature of what's happened in Germany and France in recent days."

Blunt took a deep breath. "I know you're busy, so I'll dispense with the small talk. I need a favor."

"Hopefully this isn't regarding the three Americans who were captured in Paris because I'm afraid I won't be able to help you."

"Did you read *The New York Times* article about the event?" Blunt asked.

"I did."

"And?"

"And I find it's some extraordinary propaganda."

"It's not," Blunt said flatly.

"Can you prove this?"

"Those three agents are working undercover to combat terrorism. If you reveal their names and identities, it could jeopardize their future missions."

"I appreciate your concern, Senator, but you have two problems here, starting with the fact that their images are posted at nearly all the Interpol installations throughout Europe. The second is what makes you think they're ever going to get out of prison? They committed murder on an unsanctioned hit, I'm presuming, since the State Department hasn't come to their rescue yet."

"You have to trust me on this," Blunt said. "You need to release them. Make up a story for the public that they all hanged themselves or were murdered in a prison fight. I don't care. Just let them out so they can capture Katarina Petrov."

"Katarina Petrov?" Bao asked, gasping. "Is she the one behind all this? She murdered my father."

Blunt smiled at his good fortune. "I had no idea."

"I've been searching for her more than a decade."

"If you do as I suggested, I'll make sure you get

to have a word with her before we enact justice. Does that sound like a deal you can go along with?"

Bao remained quiet for a moment. "I'll see what I can do."

Blunt hung up and waited. Less than an hour later, his phone buzzed with a major news update: Three Stuttgart Massacre Suspects Murdered in Prison.

Ten minutes later, his phone rang. It was Hawk.

"I don't know what you did, but thank you," Hawk said.

"Don't thank me," Blunt said. "Thank Jinjing Bao."

"You got the head of Interpol involved in this?"

"Turns out he has a score to settle with Katarina Petrov as well, which is kind of the deal."

"What are you talking about?"

"Bao wants a word with her before we mete out justice, considering that you find her first."

"Well, thanks to Bao we've got a chance now."

"And apparently a lead as well," Blunt said.

"How's that?"

"SnyperNet sent me some footage he scavenged from French CCTV. I'm texting you the address now of where Petrov was last seen in Paris. It's not much, but it will give you a starting place to look."

Blunt hung up the phone and sighed. He wasn't lying to Young after all.

CHAPTER 36

Paris, France

HAWK LED ALEX AND SAMUELS out a back alley and wound around the police station where they'd been held until they came to a major intersection. They took a bus back to an impound lot where they found their vehicle sitting out by the road. Hawk twirled the keys in his hand, grateful a reluctant officer on duty at the jail gave them to him. He had terse words for Hawk, who ignored the snide comments. It wasn't worth his time to explain the nuances and intricacies of his work as a black ops agent.

Once everyone piled into the car, Hawk gave the address to Alex, who plotted a course on her laptop.

"You think this will lead anywhere?" Alex asked.

"Beats any leads we had before," Hawk said.

"What makes you think she hasn't left the city

yet?" Samuels asked. "She could be anywhere in Europe by now."

"Yeah, but I know someone who knows how to contact her."

When they reached the address, Hawk parked along the curb, and then they all streamed out of the SUV. They'd arrived in an upscale burrow of Paris. Hawk knocked several times, but no one came to the door.

"Screw it," Hawk said. "We're going in."

Samuels put his hand on Hawk's chest. "You sure this is the way to go about this, big guy? I mean, after all we just went through and closed circuit cameras everywhere, you want to just kick down a door?"

"Got any better ideas?"

Samuels smiled as he pulled out his lock pick set. "I've found this is a much better way to make a discreet entry." A half a minute later, the latch clicked, permitting them access.

"Look at that," Alex said. "Brains and brawn. I had my doubts before, but I definitely think we're related."

Hawk shook his head and then put his index finger to his lips as he slipped inside. He gestured for them to split up as they all moved stealthily through the house. After they cleared almost the entire bottom floor of what looked like a three-story structure from the street, he heard a creak coming from the back entryway.

Hawk raced toward the noise and flew through the wide open door. A short stocky man sprinted away. In an effort to save time, Hawk used the railing along the steps to swing down to the ground. He raced after the man, who darted down various alleyways but failed to lose his pursuer. In less than a minute, Hawk tackled the man from behind, pinned his arms back, and then rolled him over.

"We meet again," Hawk said as he stared at Anatoly. "Why did Katarina ever leave you behind?"

"Please don't hurt me," Anatoly said. "I can explain everything."

"I doubt that," Hawk said. "But I will promise not to hurt you if you agree to help me. How's that?"

"Whatever, just please don't hit me."

Hawk slowly rose, jerking Anatoly to his feet before shoving his back toward the flat. "Why don't you begin by telling me what Katarina Petrov was doing here right after her plane was blown out of the sky? Was this some master plan of hers?"

"Of course not," Anatoly said. "She was as surprised as anyone."

"If that's so, how come she wasn't on the plane?"

"She saw you right before the plane closed its doors, and she thought better of it," Anatoly said with a faint smile. "Good premonition, eh?"

"This isn't a game. Wipe that stupid grin off your

face. Now, you said she got off the plane and then she came here."

"Yes, this is—or was—one of her homes in Paris. It wasn't her favorite, but she found it livable. I was staying here because I had to clean up the penthouse since it wouldn't be used again."

"Why not? What was she planning on doing with it?"

"Nothing, but she figured it had been burned as a legitimate hideout and didn't intend to use it again."

"What was she like when you saw her here that night?"

"She was glad she escaped but wasn't upset about what happened," Anatoly said. "She'd planned to kill them all at her Swiss chalet anyway. You saved her the trouble."

"She weaves a pretty good tale," Hawk said, seeing if he could goad more out of Anatoly.

"What do you mean?"

"I was never at the airport that night. She concocted a whopper of a story to trick you. I bet she warned you that I'd be coming for you."

Anatoly swallowed hard and nodded. "She did."

"I'm a man of my word," Hawk said. "I promised you if you helped me that I wouldn't hurt you."

"So I can go now?"

Hawk laughed. "Of course not. You're not going

anywhere until we have her in custody."

After they'd reached the back steps of the apartment, Alex and Samuels were sitting on the top step.

"Took you long enough," Alex quipped.

"Get anything out of him?" Samuels asked.

Hawk shook his head. "Working on it though."

"I don't know where she is," Anatoly said. "You're wasting your time with me."

"But you know how to reach her, don't you?"

Anatoly looked down and refused to say anything.

"It's okay," Alex said. "I know we all find it difficult to betray the people we care about and—"

"She's just my boss, okay, lady?" Anatoly said defensively.

"Whoa," Alex said. "Someone has issues. I wasn't trying to suggest anything, just that you two are close on a professional level."

Hawk snatched Anatoly's phone out of his pocket. "Give her a call. Speak quietly and tell her that we're in the room next to yours. Tell her to come over and she can take us out."

Anatoly hesitated. "I-I don't know about this."

Hawk pulled his gun out and pointed it at Anatoly's head. "What do you think now?"

"It's a great idea," Anatoly said nervously as he took the phone and dialed her number.

After he hung up and handed the phone back to Hawk, Alex nodded.

"That was clean," she said.

"She's pretty good at Russian," Hawk said. "Petrov is her mother."

"You're Alex?" Anatoly asked. "She talks about you all the time."

"Don't try to butter me up," Alex said with a glare.

Ten minutes later, there was a knock at the back door. Hawk told Samuels to answer it.

"Expecting someone so soon?" Alex asked.

"It's a favor for Blunt," Hawk said.

Anatoly strode across the hardwood floor and welcomed Petrov inside.

"What's so urgent?" she asked. "You know I need to get out of here."

Hawk slipped out of the corner and jammed his gun into Petrov's back. "Slowly, slowly," he said in Russian. "Put the bag on the ground."

Petrov followed his instructions and kept her hands in the air. "What is the meaning of this, Anatoly?"

Anatoly put his hands in the air, too. "I had no choice. They were going to kill me."

"And I'm going to kill you when this is all over with," Petrov said with a snarl.

"Good luck with that," Hawk said. "You're going to be in prison for a long time."

Samuels grabbed Petrov's wrists and bound them together with a zip tie. "We know everything. The Chamber is finished."

"You can't prove anything. And you can't take me out of this country without permission."

"Good thing they have it," came a man's voice from the top of the stairs. "Besides, we found your fingerprints on mechanisms inside the explosive devices."

Jinjing Bao descended the steps and stopped at the foot.

"As I live and breathe," he said. "You have no idea how long I've waited for this day."

"Jinjing?" Petrov said, her face turning pale. "I-I tried to call you. I-I tried to let you know. It wasn't personal. It was just—"

"You said you loved me," Bao said as he walked toward her. "Then you murdered my father and disappeared."

He recoiled and delivered a powerful blow to her stomach. "That was for my father." Then another hit. "That was for lying to me."

Doubled over in pain, Petrov tried to stand straight but struggled. "I never meant to hurt you—or fall in love."

"Save it," Bao growled.

"It started off as a job, but I swear my feelings for you were real."

Bao gestured toward the door. "Get this woman out of my sight, Hawk. I don't ever want to see or hear from her again."

Hawk grabbed Petrov's arms and shoved her toward the door. "Let's go. You've got a date with a maximum security prison, if you're lucky."

CHAPTER 37

HAWK PUT PETROV in a straightjacket once they boarded their private jet at Charles de Gaulle Airport. Cinching the drawstrings tight, Hawk showed no mercy. If Petrov lost circulation in her arm halfway across the Atlantic, he wouldn't have any pity for her. Petrov had acted ruthlessly and lawlessly—and Hawk was ready for justice to be meted out in every form as painful as possible.

A television in one corner of the plane was on where a news anchor described how a terrorist attack on Verge in Kuwait City had sent the market reeling in recent days. Hawk looked up from securing Petrov.

"There was another attack on Verge?" Hawk asked.

"That's what the man said," Samuels responded. "From the footage, it appears they got one of the main towers this time as well as several holding tanks."

"But how did they—?"

Hawk stopped and glared at Petrov. "Just another reason for me to despise you."

She smiled arrogantly. "Just blame me for everything now. If you don't like it, Petrov and The Chamber did it. Sounds about par for the course with how you Americans operate."

"We also kill terrorists who prove to be a threat to our country, which doesn't spell good news for you."

"You sure are a cocky bastard," she said. "And you don't know as much about me or The Chamber as you think you do."

"I know enough to get you convicted," he said. "That's more than enough."

"We'll see if you're still singing this same tune in a few days."

Hawk yanked on the cord, causing Petrov to wince.

Once he finished and the rest of the team was loaded on the plane, he tapped on the door to the cockpit.

"We're all set back here," Hawk said.

Nothing.

Hawk took a deep breath and exhaled. He glanced around the cabin and rapped on the door again. "Hey, Cap. You in there?"

It was quiet for a moment more.

"Sorry, I'm here," the captain finally said. "Just going through my checklist."

"Okay. Well, we're ready when you are."

"Roger that."

Hawk took a seat directly across from Petrov. "I hope this is a most unpleasant flight for you."

She frowned and shook her head. When she opened her mouth to speak, Hawk held up a device that had been sitting on the arm of his seat. "No talking—or this is going in your mouth. Understand?"

Petrov nodded.

"I'm glad we see eye to eye on that."

Hawk's phone buzzed with a number he didn't recognize.

"Hello?"

"Please hold the line for the President of the United States," came the reply.

A few seconds of silence followed by a click and then the voice of President Michaels.

"Listen here, Brady Hawk," Michaels said. "I know you probably think you're some damn American hero who deserves a parade when you get back, but I want to warn you ahead of time that nothing could be further from the truth. If you think capturing Katarina Petrov is going to exonerate you from all the sins you've committed in the name of this country, you'll be in for a rude awakening."

Hawk didn't react.

"You still there, boy?" Michaels asked.

"I know what kind of man you are," Hawk said. "I don't scare too easily, if that's what you're trying to do here."

"I'm coming for you—and you're going to rue the day you ever considered crossing me."

"I've done nothing wrong, sir," Hawk said. "But if that's how you want to play this, I'd advise you to watch your back. When you've betrayed as many people as you have, you can't always see your downfall coming."

Hawk hung up his phone as the plane lurched forward and began to roll along the tarmac.

"Was that Michaels?" Alex asked.

Hawk nodded. "That son of a bitch might be made of Teflon, but he isn't bullet proof."

Petrov smiled and raised her eyebrows in delight yet remained quiet.

"You might find this funny now, but the two of you are a pair," Hawk said. "This won't end well for either one of you. That much I can promise."

The plane came to a stop before the engines fired up and then roared down the runway, soaring upward to begin the long flight home.

Hawk couldn't wait to get back on U.S. soil—and take care of Michaels once and for all.

CHAPTER 38

Washington, D.C.

BLUNT MET THE FIRESTORM TEAM near the hangar along with several brass from the Pentagon and a dozen CIA agents. Hawk escorted Petrov off the plane and handed her over to the personnel anxious to extract information out of her about The Chamber. Hawk told Blunt they'd be fortunate to get more than her name from her. Blunt was savvy enough to know Anatoly, who the team left behind in France with Interpol agents, was the one who would sing like a canary.

After watching Petrov handcuffed in the transport van and driven away, Blunt turned his full attention to the team.

"I'm glad you all made it back unscathed," Blunt said. "You're proving to be more effective than I think anyone previously believed, myself included.

However, we still have some things we need to discuss. This way."

He gestured toward a black SUV that had the two back doors open with an agent behind the wheel.

"Who is that guy?" Hawk asked, nodding at the driver and climbing inside.

"You can trust him, Hawk," Blunt said. "He's one of the good guys."

"The list of people I trust these days has shrunk considerably."

"You're not the only one," Alex chimed in.

Once they were all inside, Blunt tapped the driver on the shoulder and the car roared to life before easing forward. In a matter of minutes, they were in stop-and-go traffic on the Beltway.

"Have you been able to keep up with the news?" Blunt asked.

Hawk shrugged. "Bits and pieces, here and there."

"I'm assuming you heard about the attack at Verge," Blunt said.

"I saw a piece about it just before we took off in Paris. Did Al Hasib do that?" Hawk asked.

"Karif Fazil, himself," Blunt said. "Video footage showed him driving the truck toward the towers, but at the last minute he dove out."

"Coward," Alex said. "I wish he would've really

gone through with the job. It'd be one less terrorist to deal with."

"Agreed," Blunt said. "However, the ramifications of a better guided vehicle loaded with explosives would've been much greater. Fortunately, Verge avoided a massive hemorrhage in its pipeline. It should return to normal within a week."

"And the market?" Samuels asked.

Blunt pulled out a cigar, clipped the end, and began to chew on it. "It's been all over the place, though I believe it's starting to stabilize now. The ultimate plan of The Chamber was to destabilize the market and influence decision makers to join Petrov's quest to create a one-world currency, but I think it's safe to say for now that she failed in that regard."

"Let's talk about the elephant in the room," Hawk said.

"Are you referring to President Michaels?" Blunt asked.

"Yeah, he's coming unhinged," Alex said. "I can't believe he was cleared."

Blunt chuckled. "Politics, dear Alex. Never underestimate the power of American politics to exonerate a criminal—or convict an innocent man."

"Or woman," she added.

"Yeah, or woman. Our political system doesn't discriminate in that regard."

"He probably has people watching us already, doesn't he?" Samuels asked.

Blunt nodded. "That's very likely. So, for now, let's lay low. I secured an apartment for the three of you near Georgetown. It's got three access points, so you can get out in a hurry if necessary."

"And three entry points for whoever wants to crash the place," Samuels said.

"We can take care of that," Hawk said.

"The place is fully stocked, and you won't have to go out unless you really want to, which I'd advise against for a few days at least. Just be careful, okay? We still have much to accomplish."

* * *

AFTER TWO DAYS, cabin fever set in for Hawk. He'd spent his downtime watching more than his fair share of Bollywood movies, while Samuels tore through several classic novels Blunt had left behind. Alex analyzed data she'd collected at various point on their last trip and tried to make sense of all the connections. But Hawk was itching to move again.

"I'm gonna go see Petrov," Hawk said.

"Are you out of your mind?" Samuels asked. "That's the last thing Blunt would want us to do."

"There are some things gnawing at me that I need to know," Hawk said. "I'll be back soon."

Alex and Samuels both pleaded with Hawk to

stay put, but he ignored their arguments. Petrov had a way of connecting with Karif Fazil. Hawk hoped that perhaps she'd have a moment of regret and want to atone for her transgressions with one final altruistic gesture. It could be a small one—the one of giving up how she contacted Fazil—but it'd be a game changer.

When Hawk arrived at the secret prison facility, he flashed his credentials to a guard who eyed him carefully.

"I don't see you on the clearance list," the guard said.

"I got this order directly from Commander Frank Stone at the Pentagon," Hawk said, tapping the desk for emphasis in an attempt to sell his bluff. "If you'd like to call Stone to confirm, be my guest."

The guard sighed. "Fine. Just sign here." He shoved a clipboard in front of Hawk, who scribbled his name illegibly on the attached paper and then gave it back to the guard. With proper authorization, the guard radioed back to another officer that Hawk was coming their way and wanted to speak with Petrov.

Hawk went through a series of metal detectors and pat downs before he arrived at the door in front of the meeting room. The door buzzed open, and Petrov was already inside, hands cuffed and attached to the table.

"What makes you think I want to speak with

you?" Petrov asked as Hawk stepped inside and the door closed behind him.

"And hello to you, too," Hawk said.

"Looking at you makes me sick," she said as she turned away and stared at the floor.

"Katarina, I work with your daughter every day," Hawk said, hoping to play on her sympathies. "I can convince her to come down here and meet you if you like. Meeting you would mean a lot to her. She has plenty of unanswered questions."

Petrov laughed and then glared at him. "Do you think your emotional mind games will work on me? I couldn't care less about Alex. She was just a means to an end, part of the assignment. That's how it was and how it always will be."

"I don't believe you," Hawk said. "I've seen how you look at her. You have questions too, don't you?"

She turned away and looked at the wall across from Hawk.

He tried a different approach. "I can make things more comfortable for you in here, maybe get you some time above the surface, outside in the sun. Would you like that?"

"I'm not interested in making any deals with you."

"Suit yourself. All I want is a way to contact Karif Fazil. After all, he's the real danger now, not you.

Are you going to let him get all the glory while you rot in this prison cell? Why not take him down with you? There's no need for you to suffer under this weight alone."

She waved him off. "Even if I told you how to connect with Fazil, he's too smart for you. He'd know something wasn't right. I know it sounds crazy, but he's got a nose for these things. He can just tell when something is wrong."

"And he'll know why now? Because you didn't send him the rest of the payment you promised him for taking out Verge? I'm sure he's pretty upset at this point."

"I don't know what you're trying to do, but if you want to get me to confess to a crime, you're going to have to be smarter about it than that. Besides, I'm still alive, aren't I? And when I get out of here, I'm coming for you."

"You're going to wish you died in here if you somehow manage to escape because I can promise you I'm not going to put you back in a cell."

She laughed. "Is that a threat or a promise?"

"If you don't want to help me, that's fine," Hawk said. "While I can make things more comfortable for you if you assist me, I can also make things more difficult if you don't. You've obviously made your choice."

Hawk stood and tapped on the door, signaling he was done. He stormed down the hall and asked for the warden to reduce her meal portions and number of showers she could have each week. It was a modest response to what she did, but it was all he had time for.

* * *

HAWK WAS ALMOST BACK to the team's apartment when his phone buzzed with a call from Alex.

"Don't worry," he said as he answered. "I'm on my way back."

"I'm glad to hear that, but that's not why I called," Alex said.

"Good because I'm in a foul mood."

"Petrov?"

"Yeah, but we'll talk about it later."

"Well, hurry back," she said. "Polat also sent another flash drive through the mail to Blunt, and I started digging through those files."

"Anything interesting?"

"Yeah, you're gonna want to see this."

CHAPTER 39

BLUNT LEAPT TO HIS FEET at the sound of his perimeter alarm beeping. Maintaining a low profile and staying off everyone's radar wasn't easy to do in Washington, but he'd managed to do so successfully for longer than he thought possible. But as he glanced as the bank of monitors from the surveillance cameras surrounding his property, he knew his run of good fortune had come to a decisive end. SWAT team members rushed along the outer wall before two of them breached the front gate. Blunt's gaze darted back and forth among the images, and he counted at least a dozen officers.

Cramming his cigar into his mouth, Blunt snatched his bottle of scotch off the counter and hobbled toward his panic room. He learned his lessons from previous secure hiding spots, having this one built with a discreet exit point a block away. If they managed to break into his panic room, he could seal himself off by ducking into a tunnel and scramble out before they could get the steel-reinforced door open. This time, Blunt had thought of everything. But he'd been around long enough to know no plan was foolproof.

Blunt watched on a laptop from his panic room as officers shouted at one another, systematically clearing each room. Access to the secret hideout came through the back of his closet by pressing a button built into the top of the doorjamb. It wasn't visible and would give the most thorough agents fits if they were determined to find a way in.

Two SWAT team members slipped into Blunt's room as he watched them on the video feed. They scoured every corner to uncover any potential hiding spots Blunt might be occupying. After a couple minutes, they left shaking their heads.

"Good," Blunt said. "You bastards get out of my house."

Blunt poured himself a glass of scotch in celebration, though he knew his house was burned. He'd have to escape to street level and find a new place, which wouldn't be easy under the current circumstances.

Blunt's phone rang with a call from an unknown number. He debated answering it for a fleeting second but knew it could be Hawk or someone else on the team with vital information.

"Hello," Blunt said.

"I'm surprised you took my call," President Michaels said.

"I don't know what you think you're doing but—"

"I'm the President of the United States. I'll do whatever the hell I wanna do. And right now, what I want to do is make sure you pay for what you did."

Blunt laughed nervously. "I wasn't the one flaunting my power in the face of the Constitution just to increase my popularity in the polls."

"And neither was I. That was about keeping America safe, nothing more."

"Just keep telling yourself that. I used to have respect for you, but now all I see is a pathetic liar who escaped the consequences of his ill-conceived actions. People died because of what you did. Their blood is on your hands."

"And you're one to talk," Michaels snapped. "I don't know where you're hiding out right now, but eventually I'm going to find you. And you're going to wish you'd never dared to challenge my authority."

"This isn't over, but I can promise you that it won't end well for you," Blunt said sneeringly.

"Besides, you have far more to lose than I do."

Blunt ended the call and removed the battery from the phone.

I'll see Michaels go down if it's the last thing I do.

CHAPTER 40

Washington, D.C.

HAWK WAS LESS THAN A BLOCK from their new safe house when he spotted two SWAT team members closing in on Alex and Samuels's location. Hawk pulled off to the side and dialed Alex's number.

"Why aren't you using the coms?" she asked. "I'm in the middle of something here."

"Listen, you two are in danger," Hawk said. "There's a SWAT team getting into position around you."

"That's the last thing I need right now."

"It's the last thing any of us need right now," Hawk said. "Michaels is on a rampage and sees us as the enemy, even though our names have been cleared. Since we haven't been technically released yet, if we're caught and dealt with, who's going to know?"

"Save your philosophical diatribes for another time," she said. "Right now, we need a way out of here."

"They're not inside yet, so do the only thing you can do at this point, pull the—"

Before Hawk could finish his statement, he heard the fire alarm going off, followed by Samuels's voice.

"Pull the fire alarm," Samuels said. "That's protocol for escaping a situation like this."

"Now, grab your stuff and get outta there," Hawk said. "I'll meet you at the rendezvous point tomorrow morning at 10:00 a.m. I would stick around and sneak you out of here, but I can't risk being seen right now."

"Roger that," she said.

* * *

THE NEXT MORNING, Hawk pulled up to the park where he'd pre-arranged to meet Alex and Samuels in the event of a separation. Hawk glanced at his watch.

Five minutes early.

But there was no sign of them anywhere. Hawk noticed a police officer scanning the area. He kept returning his gaze to Hawk's car.

Come on, come on. Where are you guys?

He wanted to call them but knew it was unwise. If there was one tenet Hawk felt was necessary to uphold in these types of situations, it was that of avoiding communication of any kind. Opening a channel to speak with Alex—whether over coms or by cell phone or text or email—could give those in pursuit the upper hand. Hawk wasn't about to risk capture because he'd arrived early and was suspicious of a cop.

The sound of a cell phone buzzing jolted Hawk.

Alex, what are you—?

He looked at his phone and saw a number appear on his screen, one that didn't belong to Alex or Samuels.

"Hello?" Hawk answered.

"Hawk, this Big Earv."

Hawk hadn't heard from Malik Earvin since Navy Seal training. Through the grapevine, Hawk had heard that Earvin left after a couple tours to join the Secret Service.

"How did you get my number?" Hawk asked, bewildered.

"I work for the president," Big Earv said with a laugh. "You don't think I can't get your number? I even know that you drank a craft beer last night. IPA, right?"

"Big Earv, I drink one of those almost every night."

Big Earv laughed. "Look, enough of the fun and games. I didn't call to catch up. I called because I need your help. *We* need your help. Your *country* needs your help."

"What are you talking about?"

"It's the president. He's been abducted."

"And there isn't anyone else better equipped to handle that than me?"

"I'm sure there is, but you know his abductor better than anyone. We could really use your help with this one."

"Who took him?"

"Katarina Petrov."

"How's that—?"

"She broke out of a secure facility last night," Big Earv said. "Apparently, she had some inside help."

"And you think I can find her?"

"Commander Stone over at the Pentagon thinks so."

Hawk glanced at his watch. It was now three minutes past ten and still no sign of Alex or Samuels.

"Okay, fine. I'll help. But I need your help too. I'm supposed to pick up a couple of team members at this park I'm at. They had to run, thanks to the FBI milling around. It's a long story and I don't want to get into it all right now, but Alex Duncan and Shane Samuels are who you need to pick up. I don't know why they're running late, but they're going to be looking for me. I'll text you the address and Alex's number. Maybe you can return the favor by keeping them safe and their whereabouts from the FBI until I get back. Sound like a deal?"

"Sending you the number of our lead agent

working the case," Big Earv said. "And I'll grab your friends for you. And, Hawk?"

"Yeah?"

"Be careful. I hear this woman is a loose cannon."

"More than you know."

Hawk peeled out of the parking lot and called the number of the Secret Service agent coordinating the recovery operation.

"Brady Hawk, boy am I glad you agreed to help us on this case," the agent said. "The last known address for them was—"

"I know where she took him," Hawk said.

"How could you? Big Earv just told you about this."

Hawk chuckled. "Yeah, but I know all about Petrov and how she operates, including her safe houses in the Washington area."

"She has multiple safe houses?"

"Yeah, but there's only one where she'd feel comfortable taking him. I'll text you the address."

"We need to know now. You can't leave us in the dark for that long."

"Do you want my help or not? I'm not inclined to tell you just so your agents can screw up the whole situation."

"Fine. Text me when you get there. I'll have a

team standing by to help."

Hawk hung up and sped toward the location he suspected Petrov would be holding Michaels at.

* * *

AN HOUR LATER, Hawk slowed down and eased to a stop along a two-lane road. Outside of the metropolis, rolling hills and old farmland made for quiet retreats for the wealthy. Blunt had once told Hawk about Petrov's old home beyond the suburbs and how she refused to sell it, renting it out through a shell corporation. Hawk learned Blunt had visited the home once when Petrov was still married and engaged in her parenting duties with Alex. Hawk concluded that if he were in a similar situation, that's where he'd go. Plenty of woods to escape into with a single approach by car to the home. And the home was so old, how many hideouts or secret passageways there were was anybody's guess.

Parking about a quarter of a mile away from the driveway, he went the rest of the way on foot. The road was quiet in the middle of the day, devoid of any traffic. A dog barked at Hawk as he crept past its house. Once Hawk cleared the fence, the yapping ceased.

Hawk decided to make his approach from below the house, which sat just at the foot of a small hill. While he wasn't sure it would make much difference,

Hawk wanted any advantage, however small it might be. If Petrov was focused on the likely route of any approaching vehicles, she might miss him. The extra time was worth the potential reward.

The house was set about three hundred meters off the road. Hawk crouched low as he hustled up toward the structure, bracing for the door to open at any second and Petrov to start firing at him. Hawk slipped up behind a felled oak tree. Part of the wood had rotted, and the grass around it had withered. The natural barrier gave Hawk a respite in his journey to the house and a chance to call Alex.

"What happened to you?" Alex demanded once she picked up. "What happened to going dark?"

"Did they pick you up?"

"Yeah," she said. "But I'm not happy about this. How come you think you can do this on your own?"

"I don't. That's why I'm calling you."

"And where exactly are you?"

"At a little country farmhouse, one I think you may have spent some time at as a kid."

"Are you at my old house?"

"I think that's where Petrov has Michaels."

"Have you confirmed that yet?"

"Not yet. That's why I haven't called the Secret Service. But I was wondering if you could give me the lay of the land so I know what I'm in for."

"Hawk, don't do this. Wait for backup. It's too dangerous to go in there alone. And if something happens to Michaels . . ."

"Nothing is going to happen to him, okay? Just tell me about the house."

She spent the next minute describing the floor plan.

"Any good hiding spots?" Hawk asked.

"There are plenty. They'd probably be too difficult to describe. But just be careful in the basement."

"Why?"

"Lots of low-hanging pipes, storage rooms, doors to the outside."

"From the basement?"

"There was a passageway from the basement to the outside that was connected by an underground tunnel," she said. "I think it was built in case of nuclear blast. There was a bunker down there for a long time, but my mother converted it into a wine cellar."

"A wine cellar?"

"I guess she knew there were no bombs coming. Anyway, that'd be a great way to get in or out, if you need to."

"Roger that," Hawk said.

"Be careful, Hawk."

"You know me."

"I do—and that's why I say that every single time."

Hawk hung up and contemplated his next move. For a fleeting second, he considered walking in the front door and leaning on his marksmanship skills but then thought better of it. The back entry was the best idea, and he knew it.

Hawk commenced to slinking around the side of the house and scanning the back for the cellar entry. It didn't take him long before he identified it and hustled toward the door. He descended the steps and found the passageway connecting the cellar to the basement.

Dangling spider webs latched on to Hawk's face as he eased through the tunnel using a flashlight from his phone for light. The dirt ground beneath him was damp and rocky, neither of which aided him in his quest to sneak in quietly.

After creeping along through the length of the tunnel, Hawk noticed a faint light coming from beneath the door leading into the basement. He took a deep breath and exhaled before drawing his weapon.

Here goes nothing.

Hawk pushed gently on the door, and light flooded into the tunnel. His eyes took a few seconds to adjust. When they did, he realized he was staring into the beams of two high wattage bulbs situated on tripods and aimed toward the door.

"I'm glad you could make it, Mr. Hawk," Petrov said as she held her gun to President Michaels's head. "I've been expecting you."

"I know you're desperate, but I don't think you fully understand what you're doing," Hawk said, keeping his gun trained on her.

"You underestimate me—*again*," she said, mocking him with her tone. "Not only do I know exactly what I'm doing, but I'm going to get you to do whatever I ask."

Hawk looked at Michaels, who had duct tape stripped across his lips. "Are you okay?"

Michaels shook his head.

Petrov waved her index finger at Hawk. "I don't think you understand who's in control here. That would be me. You don't talk to my hostage. You talk to me."

"Look, I just want to resolve this as quickly as possible without anybody getting hurt," Hawk said.

"Except for me, of course," she said. "I know you'd like to see me dead. Unfortunately, I didn't get to see the look on your face when you realized I survived your attack in Paris. Oh, it would've been priceless. But here we are."

"I don't know what your end game is, but you

need to let him go."

"Of course—in due time," she said. "But he's my insurance. You get me what I want and get me safely out of the country, and I'll make sure nothing happens to him. If not . . . boom!"

Michaels jumped a little, eliciting a squeal of delight from Petrov.

"This is going to be so much fun," she said, pulling back Michaels's blazer and revealing a bomb strapped to him.

Hawk eyed her closely, pondering how quickly he might be able to get a shot off and if it'd be true enough to kill her instantly.

"Now, I know what you're thinking," she said. "So, stop. The situation is this: I have a bomb set to detonate here on President Michaels, my once loyal subject who's become greedy recently. If I don't get your airplane and make it out of the country and back to where I need to go within the next twenty-four hours, he's going to die."

Hawk tightened the grip on his gun and took a deep breath.

"Now, you might be considering killing me, which would be a fair thought at this point," she said. "However, if I don't enter the code to kill the bomb in twenty-four hours, he dies. If he tries to remove the bomb, he dies. If he tries to defuse the bomb, he dies.

Are you starting to see a trend here? Every heroic act you might have for saving Michaels ends the same way. The only way to make sure the ending is something different is that if you give me what I want and I save his life by giving you the passcode to unlock the bomb. Make sense?"

Hawk nodded slowly.

"So, do we have a deal?"

Michaels furiously shook his head, so much so that Petrov pulled his arm behind his back and twisted it, inflicting more pain.

"No one asked you," she said as she grit her teeth. "If I don't get what I want, you die. Is that so difficult for you to understand?"

Michaels calmed down, but he shook his head imperceptibly, his eyes pleading with Hawk to refuse the deal.

Hawk thought for a few seconds. "Okay, I'll help you escape."

She smiled. "Excellent choice, Mr. Hawk, and a noble one at that. I'm sure this worthless traitor will appreciate what you did today yet try to put you behind bars tomorrow. That's just the kind of man you saved."

Hawk narrowed his eyes. "I know what kind of man he is, but I also know what kind of woman you are. If I were you, I wouldn't try to claim any moral high ground."

Petrov shrugged. "How do you Americans say it? 'To each his own?' I know who's the real criminal in this scenario."

"Let's go," Hawk said. "We don't have much time before this place will be crawling with agents. I'll have them start refueling the plane."

Hawk made a call to the airport and asked the crew to have the jet ready so they could take off minutes after he and Petrov arrived.

Petrov led them upstairs to the garage and loaded them into a four-door white sedan. Hawk still had his gun trained on her from his position in the backseat.

"You can drop the gun," Petrov said. "The only way we're all getting out of here alive is if I get what I want. Then you can get what you want. See how easy that is?"

Hawk dropped his weapon but kept it pointed in her direction—he was much more discreet about it.

"I can't believe Alex turned out so well in spite of having you as her mother," Hawk said.

"Flattery will get you nowhere," Petrov said. "Hasn't anyone told you that?"

"Just drive," Hawk growled.

"Give me your phone," Petrov said, snapping her fingers.

Hawk handed it to her and watched as she rolled

her window down and tossed it outside.

"You won't be needing that any more," she said.

Not another word was spoken until they pulled into the executive entrance at Reagan National. She eased through a security gate where the guard waved them through with barely a glance. He saluted Petrov and returned to his post.

"The Chamber has people everywhere," she said in a matter-of-fact way, almost as if she were bragging. "Every continent, every country. And, yes, before you even ask, that includes Antarctica."

Once she reached the road that ran behind all the private hangars, she turned around and looked at Hawk.

"Which way to your hangar?"

Hawk pointed left. "Number sixty-five."

She drove for just over half a mile before stopping in front of hangar number sixty-five. After she parked, she ordered them to get out of the car and then led the trio to the plane. She removed the tape from Michaels's mouth.

"Is the jet fueled and ready to go?" Petrov asked the captain standing near the steps to the cabin.

"Who is *she*?" the pilot asked.

"She's your passenger today," Hawk answered.

The pilot then realized the man was President Michaels.

"Mr. President," the captain said, "I'm sorry but

I didn't recognize you at first. Is everything okay?"

Michaels nodded and appeared to force a smile. "Just fine and dandy. Take good care of her now, will you?"

"Yes, sir," the pilot said. "You bet."

Within minutes, Petrov gave them the information they needed to file what Hawk suspected was a bogus flight plan. She handed Hawk a phone and gave him instructions for when the pilot would call him with the code to unlock Michaels's bomb vest. Then Hawk watched the plane taxi on to the runway, carrying Petrov inside.

Michaels turned to Hawk. "I underestimated you."

Hawk waved off the president. "As much as I would've preferred she put a bullet in your head, I couldn't abandon you. You're still Commander in Chief."

"And she was playing on your loyalty to your country."

"If she thought for one second that I had any loyalty to you, she would've been sorely mistaken," Hawk said.

"What's done is done," Michaels said.

"To be honest, you're not done," Hawk said, pointing to Michaels's vest. "She could still have a change in heart and let you die."

"She'll give us the code," Michaels said. "I know it."

"You have a lot more confidence in her than I do. But I guess all we have to do now is wait."

CHAPTER 41

HAWK CALLED BIG EARV and gave him an update as well as their location so the Secret Service could attend to President Michaels. While the Secret Service was embarrassed they allowed someone to kidnap the president, it wasn't their fault. Michaels admitted that he ducked his detail in order to settle a score with Petrov. According to his story, she managed to slip out of her bindings and walked out with a shiv pressed into Michaels's back. After taking a gun off one of the agents, she forced Michaels to drive her out to her old home in the country.

"You had a score to settle with Petrov?" Hawk asked. "What kind of score?"

Michaels sighed and stared at the ground.

"You're not getting out of this one. I don't care if you are the President of the United States of America, you need to talk."

"Kill me now then," Michaels said, "because I'm not telling you a damn thing."

"It's all going to come out, you know," Hawk said. "Best to be up front with the American people. They're a forgiving bunch. But try to hide something? You'll never be respected ever again."

Michaels turned his back and walked toward a row of seats in the hangar.

"Let me know when the Secret Service arrives."

Hawk watched as Michaels shuffled away. "Whatever you do, leave Noah Young alone. He's a patriot."

Michaels threw his hand in the air, giving Hawk a dismissive wave.

Hawk followed the president.

Michaels turned sharply. "Look, I'm grateful for what you did and I promise to make sure your name is officially cleared, but that's it. I don't owe you anything else, including considerations for Young. That will be between us. Got it?"

Hawk nodded, though he disagreed.

* * *

AFTER PRESIDENT MICHAELS LEFT with his security detail, Hawk called Alex and Samuels before leaving for the safe house, filling them in on all the details while driving. Once Hawk arrived, Alex nearly bowled him over when he walked through the door. He gave her a kiss before looking up to see Samuels staring at them.

"Come on, man," Samuels said. "That's my sister."

Hawk smiled and nodded. "Is this going to be

awkward for you? Because I can tell you right now that it's not changing."

"I think it's sweet," Alex said. "I never had a big brother to look out for me like that before."

"Sweetness aside, you have a choice to either fume in the corner or join us on the couch for a Bollywood movie marathon," Hawk said.

"Not before I show you something," Alex said. She tugged on Hawk's arm, leading him to the kitchen.

"Now, I'm convinced Petrov set us up with that original flash drive Polat had," Alex said. "However, he sent Blunt another one in the mail that had a few extra files on them, including some hidden folders I managed to uncover. Apparently, he was being extra careful, unconvinced he could even get this to Blunt without The Chamber finding out."

"Yet he succeeded," Hawk said.

"Yes, he did," Alex said, tapping on the keyboard. "Take a look at this."

A spreadsheet materialized on the screen that revealed a list of all The Chamber's properties and holdings. It also listed known secret agents in each country with titles and positions.

"Killing those bankers was nothing," Hawk said, his jaw going slack.

"Calling what we did the tip of the iceberg is an overstatement," Samuels said. "More like a pebble in a quarry."

"Exactly," Alex said. "But there's one name in particular I thought you might want to pay attention to."

She scrolled down and highlighted one row.

"President Michaels," Hawk said aloud. "I don't know why that doesn't surprise me."

"Makes sense now why he tried to escape the watchful eye of the Secret Service," Samuels said. "He didn't want anyone to find out he was a traitor."

"So, do you think his abduction was real or staged?" Alex asked.

"Oh, it was real," Hawk said. "Something between them went wrong. Michaels seems hell bent on killing her now, if not out of some sense of remorse, definitely out of a sense of patriotism. I think he's figured out what her end game is."

"And what is that?" Samuels asked.

"It's definitely not about money," Hawk said. "This spreadsheet shows she's got more than enough for several lifetimes."

"She's making a play for a one-world government," Alex said. "That's the only thing that makes sense."

"And once she holds the keys, all she has to do is hand them off to the Russians and we're screwed," Hawk said. "The first step is the currency, but after that, it's all downhill."

"What are we gonna do about it then?" Samuels asked.

Hawk smiled. "What do you think? We're going after her."

"And thanks to Polat, we have a blueprint for that," Alex said, tapping a few buttons on her screen to reveal another spreadsheet. "He left us a map of her daily movements and gave us suggested locations where we could ambush her and take her out."

"Let's make sure Polat doesn't die in vain," Hawk said. "And that reminds me of something."

"What?" Samuels asked.

"I need to call a certain reporter and thank him for what he did."

Hawk grabbed Alex's cell phone and called Lee Hendridge, expressing gratitude for helping clear their names in the general public.

"So, do you have any other stories for me?" Hendridge asked.

"Not yet, but we will have something soon," Hawk said. "Stay tuned. We're going to help you win a Pulitzer yet, just you wait."

Hawk was halfway through relaying his conversation with Hendridge to the team when a knock at the door interrupted them. Samuels rushed to answer it.

"It's Blunt," Samuels said as he opened the door.

With a chewed cigar hanging from his lips, Blunt lumbered into the kitchen and took a seat across the table from Hawk and Alex.

"I can't believe you saved the bastard," Blunt said. "You should've taken her out and let her shoot him."

Hawk eyed his boss closely. "That's why I'm the agent you trust," Hawk said. "If I'd let that happen . . ."

"There are probably worse outcomes," Blunt began, "but I can't think of any."

"That's not the kind of agent you hired—or the kind of man I am, not any more, anyway."

"At least you derailed her plan," Blunt said.

"For the time being," Alex added. "But it won't be long before she works to piece things back together and has a chance to push her single currency plan and put everything at risk again."

"At least now we know where she's headed," Blunt said. "No surprises now."

"So, Petrov kept her word?" Samuels asked.

Blunt sighed. "She did. The pilot relayed the code to free Michaels. But he's the least of our worries now."

"Agreed," Hawk said as he nodded. "We don't need Vice President Young to give us our next assignment. I think we all know what it's going to be."

A wry grin spread across Blunt's face. "Seek and destroy Katarina Petrov."

THE END

ACKNOWLEDGMENTS

I am grateful to so many people who have helped with the creation of this project and the entire Brady Hawk series. Morocco is one of my favorite places I've ever visited and loved setting some scenes in the book there.

Krystal Wade has been a fantastic help in handling the editing of this book, and Dwight Kuhlman has produced another great audio version for your listening pleasure.

I would also like to thank my advance reader team for all their input in improving this book along with all the other readers who have enthusiastically embraced the story of Brady Hawk. Stay tuned ... there's more Brady Hawk coming soon.

ABOUT THE AUTHOR

R.J. PATTERSON is an award-winning writer living in southeastern Idaho. He first began his illustrious writing career as a sports journalist, recording his exploits on the soccer fields in England as a young boy. Then when his father told him that people would pay him to watch sports if he would write about what he saw, he went all in. He landed his first writing job at age 15 as a sports writer for a daily newspaper in Orangeburg, S.C. He later attended earned a degree in newspaper journalism from the University of Georgia, where he took a job covering high school sports for the award-winning *Athens Banner-Herald* and *Daily News*.

He later became the sports editor of *The Valdosta Daily Times* before working in the magazine world as an editor and freelance journalist. He has won numerous writing awards, including a national award for his investigative reporting on a sordid tale surrounding an NCAA investigation over the University of Georgia football program.

R.J. enjoys the great outdoors of the Northwest while living there with his wife and three children. He still follows sports closely. He also loves connecting with readers and would love to hear from you. To stay updated about future projects, connect with him over Facebook or on the interwebs at www.RJPbooks.com and sign up for his newsletter to get deals and updates.

Made in United States
North Haven, CT
11 October 2022

25321472R00182